BRANDI

2012 GRASSIC SHORT NOVEL PRIZE

MARGARET POWERS MILARDO

EVENING STREET PRESS

DUBLIN, OHIO
EVENING STREET PRESS

Evening Street Press

December, 2012

Dublin, Ohio

Winner, Grassic Short Novel Prize 2012

ISBN: 978-1-937347-11-6

Printed in the United States of America

www.eveningstreetpress.com

10 9 8 7 6 5 4 3 2 1

BRANDI

Acknowledgements

I would like to acknowledge the debt I owe to the many professors, teachers and young people I have known over the years. Their shared experiences have helped me immensely in writing this novel. I also want to thank the Vermont Studio Center for the invaluable time I was given there to complete the first draft of *Brandi*.

PART ONE

1

"Brandi, the Freak," Denise cried out. A former student of mine, she spent many days serving in-school suspension for picking fights and for swearing at teachers and other students. Lanky, dark-haired, and strong, she typically bullied her way through school, scaring kids and fighting anyone who defied her. A good four inches taller than Brandi, Denise probably would beat her up before anyone could stop her.

Brandi said nothing in response to Denise's taunt. Instead she lunged at the taller girl. Falling to the floor in a jumble of painted fingernails and dirty shoes, the girls wrestled. Brandi, moving faster than I expected, given her bulk, gained the upper position. Sitting astride Denise, she commenced pummeling her head methodically, simultaneously bouncing on her belly. Brandi was a dirty little fighter.

"So. I'm a fuckhead?" Brandi's words came out in cadence with herbouncing. "Death to me? No way. I think. *You're* gonna die. Greaseball." On the last word, she grabbed a skein of Denise's long hair and yanked, wrenching several strands from her scalp.

"Bitch," cried Denise. Saliva sprayed from her mouth. She squirmed but couldn't dislodge Brandi. One of Denise's sneakers fell from her gyrating foot and thumped to the floor. Brandi scooped it up and tossed it toward the bystanders congregating in the corridor outside the cafeteria. A big, blond boy caught the sneaker, and a couple of other boys cheered.

Brandi held the hank of hair aloft. "Throw it," somebody called.

"Hey. Over here," another boy yelled.

"Okay, who wants it?" Brandi asked. Brandi played to her audience, who called out, whistled, and clapped in rhythm. She wound the hair into a wad, then cast it into the crowd. Blond boy caught it, and his buddies slapped him on the back.

Brandi was quite a sight. She was big: not overly tall, but hefty for her height, about five feet four. Everything about her was round. Her face was full, with big cheeks, her nose was short and, if not exactly round, softened around the edges, and even her eyes, opened wide, sat like blue M &Ms on white paper plates. Her mouth was small and pouty, her lips covered in a light shade of gloss that, amazingly, still shimmered. Her smooth-skinned face glowed pale ivory with pink cheeks and sported a few freckles across the bridge of her nose. The good looks were there, just concealed behind the weight and the ugliness of her behavior.

Brandi's arms and legs seemed shorter than they were because they were filled out with bulgy flesh, but no definition. Her thick body did not have a clear division of chest, waist, abdomen, and buttocks. All of the pieces more or less merged into one package, round and imposing. Her best feature was her hair. The color was lovely, although I wondered if she dyed it; later I learned it was natural. It was honey blond, a shimmering of various shades from very light brown to pale yellowish, the color that really looks like it was "touched by the sun." The style, if you could call it that, was stunning, as well, but in a totally contrasting way. Brandi might have been striving for the spiked look, but either the fight or no idea of how to accomplish the effect resulted in a strange hair-do. The result was a mass of uneven clumps of hair protruding from her head, some of it matted, some of it separated into strands, all of it looking less like hair than a dirty mop.

Brandi was one tough cookie. Finally Bob Lemmieux, a burly industrial arts teacher, arrived and pulled Brandi off Denise. Struggling and sniping at her captors, Brandi had a nasty word or two for the bystanders in the crowd. As she moved by me, Brandi flashed a grimace in my direction and asked, "What you looking at, bitch?"

After the crowd broke up and headed to class, I recalled a reference to her a few days prior to the fight. At the beginning of lunch period on that particular day, I had walked into the girls' lavatory. A favorite hangout, it served as an informal lounge, snack bar, and beauty salon. I found no one there but noticed a line of graffiti strung along one wall.   The words blazed in cherry-bright lipstick across the ocher cinder blocks: "Death to the Bitch--Your going to die--Brandi is a Fuckhead."

School policy required any personal threats be reported to the principal, so I had notified the office. Shocking as the words sounded, students sometimes marked up walls with nasty, cruel comments, especially if more than one person collaborated or if one kid dared another. I had wondered who this Brandi person might be that she could elicit so extreme a statement. Having just learned the answer, I realized that Denise must have been the author, and Brandi had just inflicted her style of retaliation.

2

Several weeks into the term, Brandi transferred to my teaching team. She always dressed in jeans. At school there was a sort of teen-age fashion cult concerning the proper design, fabric, color, and accessories for jeans. Despite her extra weight, Brandi was as conscious of the style as any girl her age. She owned a wardrobe of jeans that ran the gamut of adolescent fashion-consciousness: flares, bells, straight legs, baggies, low-risers.

As for her tops and her shoes, Brandi also showed herself a savvy dresser. The tops hung loose, in an attempt to hide her bulk, and were either sweaters or of jersey material. She wore both short-sleeved and long-sleeved tops, mostly in pale or, more likely, just faded colors: light blue, beige, lavender, green. She also owned the inevitable gray sweatshirt; she could wear that over anything, and it served as a sort of uniform for both boys and girls-- jeans and a gray sweatshirt, a safe, blend-into-the-crowd kind of outfit. Although she owned acceptable Nikes, she preferred a pair of black leather platform shoes with laces and rounded toes. They increased her height at least two inches.

Each day in class I never knew what kind of mood Brandi might be in or how she would act. Some days she arrived sullen and remained quiet and distant for the entire class, though these occasions happened infrequently. More commonly she stormed into the room, her voice leading the way. Discord and unpleasantness followed her, then hung, cloud-like, over her head, a personal little storm.

At rare times she entered the room calmly, like most of the kids. One such day I instructed the students to write a personal narrative. "You're not going to make us read these out loud, are you?" Brandi asked. When I assured her that only I would read the essays, she immediately set to work, writing for most of the class time. When she finished her composition, Brandi set down her pencil and lay her head on the desk. I left her alone until I called for the papers.

Rising, she handed me her narrative without saying a word and left the room.

I forgot about her paper until the evening, when I was reading her class's work and picked hers from the pile:

> Each day I wake up and wonder will any body appreciate me for who I am. Thats the question! I look at myself in the mirror. Reflecting off me is a person wanting high education. I look at myself and wonder am I any good for someone. I look at other girls my age always trying to be like them. Wanting to be cool in my own way. Every time I look at myself striving to be better each day. Taking nonsense and sense and putting it together and becomes a life for others. I wonder will I be like them? I know that each day I get up and go to school. Everybody makes fun of me always saying there better than me. Maybe they are. I want to go to collage and my years in school are going fast. I know I'll be what I am forever. I'll be that person wanting more in my life. Will I ever get married or live in a rich mansion? No one can predict the future. But I know that if I was pretty and popular, guys would like me. I know somewhere there is a person just perfect for me. I wonder will I ever go to the prom or be popular?

Setting the paper on my desk, I thought about the disparity between Brandi the thick-skinned tough and Brandi the insecure twelve-year-old. A sensitive girl dwelled in there somewhere, and I vowed to scratch the surface to find out who appeared.

I returned to school after Thanksgiving vacation, but Brandi did not.

After three days, the seventh grade guidance counselor, Elaine Fowler, informed me that Brandi had run away from home. The parents did not know where she was, and, according to the counselor, they probably wouldn't look for her because, "She's run off in the past and always come back when she's ready." Elaine guessed that she had gone to Portland and joined the fairly large number of adolescent runaways who lived on the street, panhandled, and visited the soup kitchen for one meal a day.

"How will you find her?" I asked.

"Hey, the parents don't care. I tend to agree with them. She'll show up when she's ready.".

"Well, don't you have to report this to the authorities? Doesn't the school have a responsibility for her safety?"

"I've contacted the Department of Human Services. They take it from there--at least till she returns. Then we'll have to meet with the DHS caseworker, her parents, maybe a social worker and a psychologist, the whole nine yards."

"It seems so cold-blooded to let a twelve-year-old child fend for herself like that..." I began.

Elaine cut me off. "Hey, nobody permitted her to go--she took off herself. Besides, this kid is a pain to everybody. She made it clear she has no use for us. I've got plenty of good kids who appreciate what I try to do for them. Besides, I say good riddance to bad rubbish." She turned from me and headed toward her office.

I taught my classes, noting each day that Brandi did not return. I knew I would hear from the principal when he got any news about her. As Christmas break approached and still Brandi had not appeared at school, I wondered what she was doing.

3

School resumed in January, and Brandi continued to remain among the missing. At the end of the month she returned, without fanfare. On a Thursday she sauntered into my classroom to a cacophony of comments and questions from the other students.

"Hey, look who's back."

"Wow--where ya been, man?"

"Geez, I thought you were the smart one. But you came back, dummy.

What'd you do that for?"

"Lookin' good, lady, lookin' real good." This comment came from the loud mouth of Kevin Wiley, a big, heavy-set boy descended from a long line of woodsmen. He considered school a place to park himself until he turned sixteen. Kevin often waxed eloquent on the relative merits of chain saws, splitters, skidders, and cherry pickers, while he kept one of his pale green eyes perpetually focused for attractive girls.

Brandi's appearance startled me as much as it did my students. I was surprised by her return to school, more surprised by her looks. She was noticeably thinner, twenty pounds thinner, I guessed. With bulk reduced, her body had definition: hips, waist, and breasts. The round face had disappeared, replaced with more of an oval; high cheekbones stood out, and her lips appeared fuller. Her eyes sparkled as before, although they took on more prominence in the slimmer face. Somebody had styled her hair, which practically squeaked of clean and lay over her head in short, loose curls. The morning sun caught the golden highlights.

Brandi strutted in new clothes that fit properly and looked good. She wore jeans, a traditional cut that neither bagged nor trailed on the floor. Her shoes were black platforms with laces, but lower and less clunky than her old ones. A long-sleeved, light blue sweater enhanced the blue of her eyes and contrasted nicely with the red-gold of her hair. Brandi looked pretty.

The class thought so, too. I noticed them watching her while she walked across the room to my desk. "Hey, Ms. M., I'm here."

Both the boys and the girls were curious about the "new" Brandi. Everyone, it seemed, wanted to know where she'd been, what she'd been doing, what was going on.

"You been gone so long, I thought you died. Ha. I guess you didn't though."

"Somebody told me you been in Portland. I bet you ain't been nowhere. You just been home playin' hooky."

"You really been livin' on the street?"

"What's it like?"

Fascinated by her unexpected disappearance, her classmates asked if Brandi could share her experience of running away and living on her own. I asked Brandi if she wanted to tell us what had happened to her. She shrugged and said, "Okay," but I thought her smile belied the blasé response.

Most of the students wanted to hear Brandi's story. I anticipated many questions, so I told the class to save comments and questions until Brandi finished talking. Apparently enjoying the attention, she spent the better part of two classes talking. I got as caught up in the story as the kids.

"I been livin' on the street in Portland. It's a great way to lose weight. Maybe you wanna try it, Ms. M.

"Really, though, I don't recommend it. It's pretty hard. I was cold most of the time. There was about six of us who hung together. We'd sleep at the Y, but ya can't go there before eight at night, and ya gotta be out at seven. The library is warm, but we'd get thrown out after about an hour.

Dunkin' Donuts lets kids hang there when it's not busy, but you can only stay there for a little while. Then you gotta move on and come back later. Same with the library. We'd go back a lot. But people in the library don't like us. 'That element,' they call us. The bitchy ladies claimed we messed up the place. Sometimes they didn't let us stay a whole hour at a time.

"You can go to the soup kitchen once a day for lunch," Brandi was telling the class. "Anything else ya eat is what ya can cop. It's pretty easy to take stuff from some places. Some stuff is easier to lift, too. I ate candy, but it's hard to get bread--it don't fit in your pocket very well--and lunch meat and cheese, stuff like that's almost impossible. They watch that stuff like a hawk."

No wonder she'd lost so much weight, I thought--one meal a day and what food she could steal.

"People rip each other off a lot," she said. That's why you join a family. There's at least one big guy—it's better if there's two-- so other families give you space. There's a couple other kids who can take care of themselves," Brandi smiled and pointed her thumbs toward herself. "Then you take in a couple of babies, kids who'd never make it without protection. One time I ripped off a leather coat from this dude. He was a real mean sucker, but I got it when he was passed out. Mike took it away from me, though.

"Mike's a cop--the best. He took away Rafe's leather jacket from me because he said, when Rafe saw me with it, he'd cut me bad for sure. Then he got me a new coat. He bought it with his own money. And he's got kids of his own to take care of. But they're all boys. He said he liked me cuz I got 'potential.' The jacket's cool. It's in my locker—I'll wear it to next class."

Brandi said that sometimes Mike bought her supper. He'd take her to Reilly's, a favorite diner for Portland police, and buy her burgers and fries. "Some of the cops used to rag him that I was his penance. I don't know what that meant. This one nasty cop, Steig, said I was his whore--sorry, Ms. M., but that's a quote. It's not true, though. Mike's married and has a beautiful wife. I saw her once. He introduced me to her, and she was real nice. Mike is just a great cop.

"I wasn't gonna come back. Even if it's tough on the street, at least there ain't a lotta dumb rules, people makin ya do stupid stuff, and school. It got so cold, though, that I went to the children's shelter. Then I found out ya can't stay more than two weeks. The DHS butts in and takes ya away. And I've had enough of goin' to foster homes where all they want is the money and the hell with you. They said I'd better figure out if I wanted to get sent up by DHS or go back home voluntarily. I didn't volunteer—ha, ha—but I decided to come back."

Staying on the street all winter became too dangerous. Brandi said one boy she knew got so sick that he was hospitalized and almost died. Several students acted worried and vocalized their concerns.

"Did the shelter ever get full?" Ethan asked. Normally spaced out or reading one of his fantasy books during class discussions, Ethan had been unusually attentive to Brandi's tale.

"Sometimes it did, yeah--especially when the weather got bad," she answered.

"Well, what did kids do then?" Ethan's frown revealed his interest.

"Tough it out, mostly. I got closed out one night with a couple other kids. We found some cardboard and old newspapers, junk like that, and holed up under the old Million Dollar Bridge. That's where the winos and some of the heavy-duty streets live..."

"Ah, that's not true. Nobody would live outside under a bridge in the winter," cut in Andy, an only child of professional parents and, from all I knew of the family, a boy who was loved, coddled, and indulged with designer-label clothes, gadgets, and trips to Florida and the Caribbean.

"A lot you know about the real world, Demers," scoffed Brandi. "Not everybody works or makes a lot of money."

"What was it like under the bridge?" Jessica looked up from the notebook she was writing in. "How did the people keep warm?"

"There's rocks, huge chunks of broken concrete, brush under there.

"People dragged in lots of pieces of wood, tin or some kind of metal, and boxes from refrigerators and stuff that they've built into these huts, sort of. They started fires in metal barrels or inside piles of rocks. We couldn't go near them, but they didn't bother us if we brought our own junk and set it up away from them.

"Anyway, before DHS brought me back, they got me some new clothes, too. The social worker lady was pretty cool. We went to the Mall, and she helped me pick out stuff. Then we went to Regis, and both of us had our hair cut. She paid for that herself.

"So, here I am."

Here she was indeed, I thought--something of a heroine to many of the students, an alien to others.

4

By state law the school would help make any decisions about Brandi after her return. The guidance office set up Brandi's Pupil Evaluation Team Plan (P.E.T.) for late winter. That's when I had my first, and only, opportunity to meet her parents, all four of them. Brandi divided her time between her mother and her step-father, Mrs. and Mr. Barrett, and her father and her step-mother, Mr. and Mrs. Robb.

Brandi's mother was a small woman with nondescript features and light hair. I guessed her age to be about forty. Her husband, an attractive blond with an easy smile, seemed quite a bit younger. I learned that Mr. Barrett had full custody of his two children from a previous marriage, a boy of eight and a five-year-old girl. Brandi lived with them off and on after their marriage two years before, but the Barretts had put her out in the fall. Now she lived with her father and her step-mother.

Mr. Robb seemed considerably older than Brandi's mother, perhaps fifty.He was short and heavy, with dark hair balding on top. His wife was of an indeterminate age; she looked as if she'd led a hard life. A couple of her teeth were missing, her skin was mottled, and her clothes were shabby.

During the conversation, I discovered that Brandi had been adopted when she was very young; thus, all four people discussing her future were not related to her by blood. Furthermore, she had spent several periods of time, totaling close to three years, in foster homes in Southern Maine. Mr. Robb and Mrs. Barrett, when still married to each other, sent her away because they thought Brandi was "disruptive" to the household. Their other children were older, they all worked, and she demanded too much of their time and attention. She acted "spoiled and fresh," according to her mother.

After the breakup of their marriage, the adoptive parents took turns keeping Brandi, a week or two with one, then a week or so with the other.

When she became difficult to deal with, they put her in foster care. Now that Mr. Robb had remarried, he and his wife decided to try again. Mrs. Robb was home most of the time, and Brandi's father worked sporadically, so they had more time to spend with her.

Mrs. Barrett said she doubted the situation would work. She refused to have Brandi visit her house after the run-away incident but expressed her willingness to let the Robbs do whatever they thought they could. "I don't think you can handle her," she said, looking down the table in the direction of Mr. Robb. "You couldn't before, but go ahead and try."

Mr. Robb said that things were different now. Mrs. Robb added, "He's trying very hard with her. We both are." Mrs. Barrett said nothing more; she seemed to be disinterested in the remainder of the meeting. Mr. Barrett smiled a lot and nodded his head occasionally, but he never spoke.

The P.E.T. meeting ended after an hour that included a review of the objectives of the past year, a discussion of the progress, or lack of, over the past year, and a set of expectations for completing the year. I left the meeting unclear where the girl Brandi fit into the plan outlined by the social worker, the school psychologist, an administrator, the teachers, and Brandi's legal guardians. Previous to the P.E.T. meeting, I knew she had two sets of parents, but I had not known that she was adopted. I wondered how much, if anything, she knew about her biological parents and if it made any difference to her.

5

Toward the end of a school year, I usually asked my students to keep a writing journal. The writing could be about anything: personal thoughts, complaints, stories, poems, a daily schedule of tasks. I checked to make sure they wrote each day, but I didn't read the journal unless invited to do so.

Brandi told me she planned to use her journal to keep a record of her romances. Since her return to school after running away, she had begun dating and spending time with different boys. Her weight loss and new habit of cleaning and primping herself had attracted a following of seventh and eighth grade boys. A couple of the high school boys sometimes drove her to school and picked her up afterwards. Brandi's attendance had improved as a result of all this attention.

One morning about a week before school let out for the summer, she entered the room, appearing agitated. She came in with her head down, shuffled her feet, and looked a little shaky. Her face was blotchy, her eyes were red, and her tank top was ripped at the shoulder. I asked her what had happened.

"Nothin!" She emitted a long pause, then a sigh. "Everything sucks."

"Do you want to talk about it with anybody?"

"Naw. Nobody can help."

"How about writing about it?"

"That's gay. What good's it gonna do?"

"Maybe none. But maybe it will take some of the pressure off. Blow off some steam on paper, and maybe doing that will make you feel better."

"It won't. Believe me."

Brandi sat at her desk brooding for a while. She tapped a couple of fingers of one hand on the back of the other hand. Eventually she got out her journal--a loose-leaf notebook she had covered with pictures of male movie stars and models and decorated with different shades of nail polish.

For the remainder of class, she wrote. Every time I glanced at her, she was busy pushing her pencil across the page. Great, I thought . It seemed to be calming her..

When the bell rang, she rose, walked to the door, and thrust the notebook at me. "Here. You can read it if you want. You don't have to, though. It's stupid."

I said thank you, but she'd already left the room and was headed along the hall at a fast pace.

At the end of the day I had a break and opened Brandi's journal to read:

> When I started school after vacation, I was having problems and started to drink again and overdose and other stuff. I had gotten adicted and I couldn't stop. Until that is when I got realy sick and dizzy and passed out at my friend Deans house. I felt weird when I had woke up. To my surprise he never told anyone.
>
> It might change my life If I didn't overdose because I would not be so different and would not be so against others so much. I only

rember a few things from when I was as normal as everyone else. They was before my mother died. I was practically only a baby when she left. I kind of miss blending in with the crowd.

Now its different. I go to school and get in trouble and have no Idea why. It makes me feel stupid when people come up to me and say what did you do this time or something like that.

Sometimes I look in the mirror and question who or what is looking back. Sometimes I wonder why anyone is my friend when I cant even figure out who I am. I mean why does anyone care anyway about what I do to myself when they don't even know me as me. I wish that I was never adicted and never started. Nobody trusts me and I have headacks and I don feal very well. But I cant stop. Thats why I went to the school drug and alcohol counsuler. He started to help me but then I got kicked out of school so I had noone to talk to about this problem. So I want to change but its impossible.

I barely had put down the journal when I heard my name called on the school intercom to report to the clinic.   I started across the courtyard between the buildings and noticed a rescue van parked near the main entrance. Two volunteers pushing a gurney rushed by me into the clinic. Brandi lay on one of the beds. The rescue crew bundled her onto the gurney while Mrs. Chambers, the school nurse, hovered nearby. As I watched, the clinic aide told me that Brandi had "ingested an undetermined substance" she apparently had hidden in her backpack. Some girls found her lying on the floor in an eighth grade lavatory.

She did not return for the final week of school.

Several times over the summer, I was preoccupied with thoughts of Brandi. Sometimes I wondered if her essays were more than just journal writings.   Perhaps she put down things that troubled her, or maybe she wrote what she did for the shock value.

Maybe she wanted me to respond differently from the way I had. I hadn't done much to help. I wondered if, when she'd left my room after handing me her journal that day, she'd gone to the bathroom and taken the drugs then.

Although my thoughts dwelled on her, I didn't do anything about it that summer. I rationalized that somebody else would help her.

PART TWO

1

School started at the beginning of September, and I was caught up in the frenzy of new students, paperwork, goals for the term, and the general excitement of another school year. Although her seventh grade record was poor, Brandi had not failed any courses, so she was promoted. I lost track of her for a while after she entered the eighth grade.

Early in October, I learned from an eighth grade teacher that Brandi's promotion was accompanied by a confidential report that cautioned teachers to use care with her. Considered a negative influence and a possible danger to others, she quickly became notorious, and several teachers singled her out as the major problem student for the year.

Brandi had been involved in a couple of fights, one where the other girl required stitches at the emergency room. She was sent home and suspended, but the other girl's parents threatened to file charges. The details I gleaned about the incident were sketchy because the administration had cautioned the staff not to speak to anyone about Brandi.

I knew that she returned to school after the suspension because she came to visit me one afternoon in late October. She was taller, and her hair had a blousy look to it. One big difference I noticed was that she was wearing a black turtleneck. In the past I had never seen Brandi wear either black or a turtleneck. When I commented on her change of style, she pulled the top of the jersey away from her neck, and I saw purplish blotches. "How did you get those terrible bruises?" I asked.

"I tried to hang myself."

"Oh," I said. Brandi never failed to surprise me, and I felt at a loss to help her.

"What happened?"

"The rope broke."

In the course of our conversation, she told me that she got "tired of staying home." One day when she was alone in the trailer, she got some rope, threw it over a metal beam, and made a loop. She stood on a chair and jumped off. The rope caught around her neck for a few moments, then broke, and she fell to the floor. Brandi laughed and said, "When my dad got home, he took me to the hospital. They made me go to the loony bin for ten days. I had to meet with a shrink, take tests, and go to group therapy. What a drag. But things are better now."

After she left, I kept seeing the image of an unhappy kid hanging by her neck from a piece of dirty cord that she swung over the ceiling beam of a squalid trailer rusting away in some crummy scrub area outside of town. What desperation leads a thirteen-year-old to attempt ending her own life?

Despite her bravado, things apparently did not improve for Brandi. She skipped classes regularly, and at least a couple of her teachers preferred she do so; then they did not have to deal with her. She enjoyed wandering the halls "intimidating nice kids", as one teacher phrased it. Another of her pastimes was to hang out in one of the lavatories and surprise some unsuspecting girl sitting in a stall. The year before she told me about these shenanigans herself, during one of the many times we shared lunch "detention" in my classroom. At a delicate moment, she would bound over the top of the stall and deposit a portion of the toilet's contents--wadded paper, a used tampon, even feces--over the girl's head. When I asked her why she did this, Brandi told me, "Well, I don't bother nobody that don't mess with me. But if a bitch has fucked with me, then she better watch out. Cuz I don't take shit from nobody. I give it to 'em. Get the joke? Ha."

Just before Christmas, Brandi finally tried the patience of the administration one time too many. The Friday before vacation, the Student Council sponsored a dance for seventh and eighth graders, planned for after school. Anybody who had a written note from a parent could stay after school and ride an activity bus home. The Parent Council was providing refreshments: punch, chips, and popcorn balls. During morning classes, Brandi stopped by her locker several times, both with and without permission.

Around ten-thirty, on a tip from the boyfriend of one of the "bitches" she periodically teased, the assistant principal examined Brandi's locker. He confiscated some unopened condoms, three single-edge razor blades, and a fifth of vodka, not quite two-thirds full. When she was questioned by the principal, the substance abuse counselor, and the campus policeman, Brandi said she was keeping the condoms for a boy who asked her to hold them for her until after school. The razor blades she was planning to use at the end of the day to do her hair in a shag for the dance. She needed three blades because her hair was "coarse, and I want the ends to be done crisp, like."

As for the vodka, "It's for a party tonight; I'm taking it to a guy for a Christmas present. I had to bring it to school cuz I'm not going home in between." If it was a present, the substance abuse counselor asked, why was it opened and a third of the contents missing. "Ah, com'on, Mr. Sy, you know this dump is a drag. And Mrs. Hough really has the rag on today. She started in on me even before I breathed on her, for crists sake. I just wanted to take the edge, off--ya know, feel good?"

She was suspended, but the administration had to keep her under their supervision until the end of the day because neither her father nor her mother could be reached. Every student had on file an emergency card listing the names of two adults, neighbors or relatives, who could be called when the parent was not available. At one of the places, no one answered the phone, and, at the other listing, the phone had been disconnected.

Brandi left on the bus at the end of the day and did not come to school again before vacation.

Christmas break lasted two weeks, and basically I forgot about Brandi. She crossed my mind now and then, but I did not put any thoughts about her into action.

When classes resumed, she remained at home, since the school board had suspended her indefinitely, thus making her father, Mr. Robb, and his wife responsible for her daily supervision. A tutor went to the house three times a week for two hours each visit. The authorities, including the school administration, the guidance counselor, the substance abuse counselor, the campus police, and a DHS representative, met to discuss a long term plan for Brandi, including the conditions of her return to school.

In the meantime, I learned through the school grapevine that Brandi had free rein, using her father's home as a base to host parties, often with boys who either were on suspension or who skipped classes to visit the Robb's trailer. She provided an occasional bottle of hard liquor and a place to crash. The boys sometimes brought beer, liquor, pot, or pills.

One of the days that some high school boys came to see her, she suggested they go to the mall, saying she had shopping to do. She may have done some legitimate shopping, but Brandi was stopped by a Macy's security guard and found with several pieces of jewelry, unpaid for, in her possession. The store refused to handle the situation with leniency, especially after Brandi "decked the stupid bitch," as she told me when I saw her at the State Youth Detention Center in late January. "The bitch put her fuckin' hands on me. And you know, Ms. M., anybody touchin' me makes me crazy. What'd she think? She shouldna put her crummy hands on me."

I found out that the female security guard weighed about a hundred pounds soaking wet and was three months pregnant at the time Brandi assaulted her. The woman suffered several cuts and bruises, although the baby was not injured. Brandi was sent to the Youth Detention Center until her hearing. Due to the poor economic situation in the state, staffing shortages in the Department of Human Resources, and the general inattention paid to youthful offenders without parental clout or financial means, Brandi was likely to languish at the Detention Center for two or three months until her case came up for review.

2

Cutbacks in funding by the State Legislature and negative publicity about overuse of a disciplinary tactic called the "time-out restraint chair" had lowered staff morale at the Youth Detention Center. The ratio of teachers to students was below standard levels. Many of the students had special needs, such as learning disabilities, speech and hearing impairments, and psychological disorders, but professional services for these youth were limited. Girls, representing a small proportion of the Detention Center residents, received lower quality services than boys. Some people who had experience with the education program labeled the Center a "throw-away school for throw-away kids."

Fortunately, Brandi qualified for tutorial help through a program in our school system. Her eighth grade teachers declined the dubious honor of tutoring her, so I accepted the assignment to work with her three times a week, after the regular school day. It seemed like a good way to get involved with her again and maybe help.

I'd driven by the Youth Detention Center for years, but I'd never been inside before. The complex sat atop a rise of land adjacent to the interstate highway, close to the airport, and within sight of the city and the bay. Originally a working farm, the Detention Center still had a few farm buildings remaining and a lot of open space. Several small buildings, called cottages, housed the detainees. The only outward sign that the place restrained people was the high metal fence enclosing the Center. Nearby residents had complained that youths could walk off the grounds at will, endangering others, so the state erected the fence. In fact, some of the detained youths, mostly boys from upcountry, periodically escaped and stole cars, usually in an attempt to get home.

After Brandi had been at the Youth Detention Center for about two weeks, I made my first visit. I met her in a central lounge area in one of the main buildings. She was accompanied by a beefy woman who, I guessed, weighed two hundred pounds. Bosoms large enough to create a single protruding shelf pushed the bodice of her green shirt until spaces gaped between the buttons. A plastic name badge, pinned over the left breast, said, "Muriel." Her frame was solid, yet pudgy around the waist, thighs, and upper arms, where the fabric of her uniform strained at the seams. The visible skin on her arms and face was ruddy, the way harsh laundry soap or overexposure to chill winds reddens and roughens normally pale skin. Her eyes were brown, and her hair, a brassy blond color, was done up in a bun at the base of her neck. The woman nodded as I walked into the room but did not speak.

"Hey, Ms. M. What're you doin here?" Brandi sprang from a chair she was slouched in and reached me in a couple of bounds. I noticed her bare feet.

Instinctively opening my arms to embrace her, I remembered she was the girl who warned that people "should keep their crummy hands off me." But she stepped into my hug, wrapping her arms around me. I held on to her a few moments. She broke the embrace, stood back, and said, "Yo, what's up?"

"I'm planning to be your tutor for a while, if that's okay with you."

"Cool, Dude. I tell ya, the teachers here, they don't know shit. How come you're coming here--the school makin' you do it?"

"I'm getting paid, but I volunteered to tutor you."

She looked at me for a minute, her face set at a tilt, eyes holding mine, lips pursed. Then her mouth split in a big smile, and she broke into a hearty laugh. "Well, okay. I can handle that. It's so fucking boring here, anyway."

"Today, I thought we'd just sort of visit. I can find out what you've been doing here and tell you what's going on in class. I'd like to see your room, too, if that's all right with you."

"Yeah, well, you can see my room. I've been moved from my old one. My first roommate was a fuckin' psycho. All she did was cry, throw things, and write to her boyfriend. He's up at Wardham. He got sent there for the gig they pulled--beat up an old lady and stole her money. The old lady was her grandmother or great aunt, something like that. The cops got 'em the next day-- what a couple of morons, huh. She's the same age as me, so she got sent here. Since he's twenty-two, he got real time at Wardham. I've got a new roommate now--she's nuts, too," she said, glancing toward Muriel and scowling.

By the door Brandi stepped into her sneakers, minus their laces. "They think I might try to hang myself with the laces of my Nikes. That's so gay. Besides, you know I've already done that." Laughing, she stepped outside without putting on a jacket. Muriel came out and closed the door behind us. "Don't pay any attention to Matron Muriel the Mute Mule," she told me. "She thinks she's a keeper in the zoo---aaugh." She turned and stuck out her tongue at the woman, who ignored her.

Before I came to see Brandi, I learned that she had been labeled dangerous to others, even in a place that housed some of the state's more violent adolescents. One of the first days at the Detention Center, she fought with another girl, whose arm was broken in the fight. A second fight, with a boy, resulted in another injury, this time from a knife. Brandi claimed the knife belonged to the boy, who attempted to stab her, and, in wrestling it away from him and defending herself, she cut him accidentally.

Regardless of whose knife it was, the staff director decided she was a menace to others at the Center. He assigned her to a room of her own in one of the cottages located in an isolated section of the campus. Muriel Buckman, a matron experienced in dealing with violent adolescents, shared the room and accompanied her wherever she went.

When we set off along a winding pathway toward the cottage, Muriel followed a short distance behind, pacing herself so that she remained out of earshot of our conversation but within sight of us. The building was a small wooden structure that resembled a modular house more than a cottage. The front door opened into a common room. Two bedrooms and a bathroom opened off that room. The linoleum floor had a few small rugs scattered on it. There were a couple of vinyl upholstered couches in the room, as well as a table and four straight chairs. While everything looked cheap, the place was immaculate. The walls appeared to be freshly painted, a pale green shade. When I commented on the cleanliness, Brandi remarked, "Yeah, they use slave labor here. Old Mute Muriel cracks the whip, and I have to clean or else get beat up."

"Oh, really?" I asked, catching the matron's eye. She shook her head once but remained silent and seemed composed in spite of Brandi's comments.

"Wanna see my room--whoops, our room?" Brandi asked. When I nodded, she opened a door and entered a small room that was as clean as the common room but not as neat There were clothes scattered on one of the beds and over the arm of a chair, and books and papers littered a small desk. The beds were covered with plaid spreads that matched the curtains on the one window. Other than the few clothes and the papers, the room had an impersonal look about it.

"Okay, Muriel-babe, butt out. Me and Ms. M. are gonna chill for a while--and you're not invited. In fact, why don't you make yourself useful and get us a couple cokes? Ha, ha. Don't worry. I'm not gonna cut her--she's cool."

Muriel did not get us cokes, but she allowed us to be alone for about half an hour. She left the bedroom door ajar on her way out to the common room where she settled her bulk onto one of the couches and read a magazine.

When I told Brandi about school, she seemed interested, asking about certain people, making comments about others. She told me I was her first visitor. "How about your family--your father or your mother?" I asked.

"Oh, no way. My father's been on a bender for weeks, and my mother said she's finished with me--I disappoint her." She rolled her eyes.

"How do you feel about that?"

Looking at me, she said, "Don't get mental on me, Ms. M. If you wanna read books and do school stuff and shoot the shit, fine, but, if you're gonna start actin' like one of the shrinks, don't bother to come."

Depending on how I responded, I sensed I might be able to develop a relationship with Brandi or I could end our contact right then.

"Okay, kiddo," I said. "Sorry."

"No problem."

By the time our visit ended, Brandi and I had decided to read a book together when I returned in a couple of days--I'd brought along two copies of *Emmeline.* In the meantime, she said she would write something for me. "The shrink wants me to keep a journal. I told him I ain't showin' it to nobody. But I'll let you see it, if you want."

I said it would please me if she let me read something she wrote.

Rummaging through the papers on her desk, she came up with a single sheet of lined notebook paper, folded it into quarters, and handed it to me, saying, "Don't read it till after you go, okay?"

"Okay."

Late that evening, I took out the paper Brandi had given me and read it:

> My mother's name is Barbara Richardson. She died on June "6, 1989 at 9:06 p.m. She died of canser. She died in a hospitle far away from me. I was only four years old at the time and ever sence that night, my life has been very hard. I lived with all different people and at times its really nice but other times its not so nice. Like when I need a woman and a friend to talk to. I always think about my wedding day and how she won't be there. I don't remember her much and that's what kills me the most.

Now I knew another piece to the puzzle that was Brandi. So she did know about her real mother and maybe even remembered her a little bit. And what about her father? Did she know who he was? How much did this loss affect her attitude and contribute to her unsavory behavior, I wondered.

3

Two days later a gray sky spit snow, and a stiff wind whipped it around before it fell on the ground, covered already with several inches of fresh snow from a storm the day before. Brandi was waiting for me when I drove into the parking lot. She stood at the end of the walkway, her hands under the armpits of the shapeless sweater she wore, no coat and no mittens. She had on the lace-less Nikes, which were wet through from the snow. Muriel, dressed in a heavy jacket, boots, hat, and gloves, was standing several yards back on the walkway.

As I opened the car door, Brandi came alongside and said, "I thought you might not come."

"I said I would."

"Yeah, but, ya know, you got a lotta things to do and stuff. I know you're busy and all."

"If I tell you I'm coming, I'll be there. Unless it's an emergency, and then I'll call. So, how are you?"

"Okay. Hey, I read that book. There's nothing to do around this dump. That girl, Emmeline, sure had it tough. What a stupid thing to do—marry your own kid."

"But she didn't know he was her son. She was raped when she was twelve. Then the baby was taken from her, and she never saw him. In fact, she didn't know if the baby was a boy or a girl. It was years later when she met him as a grown man, and she never knew who adopted him or what his name was."

"Well, it's pretty dumb. Nothing like that happens in real life."

"Actually, the novel is based on a true story. The girl supposedly lived in Fayette, Maine, and was sent by her parents to work in the textile mills in Lawrence, Massachusetts. Young girls were recruited from poor rural families in Northern New England because they provided cheap labor for the mills, and the family received a portion of the daughter's wages and one less mouth to feed."

"Oh. Well, I'm glad there aren't no mills like that anymore. My mother would've been glad to get rid of me that way if she could. But I wouldn't of been stupid enough to let some rich guy rape me. I'd of killed him first."

By this time we had arrived at the cottage and settled ourselves on the couches, while Muriel went into the bedroom, leaving the door open. Facing away from us, she sat at the desk and began writing.

Brandi and I talked about the book a little more before we shared events of the last two days. Nothing of any note had happened to either of us. Since she could not leave the Detention Center, I'd arranged to bring some movies we could watch together. The administration had set up a T.V. and a V.C.R. in the common room of the cottage. We spent the last half hour watching part of a movie. When I left the Center, I gave her a set of questions about the movie and about *Emmeline* to write on for our next meeting. She walked me to my car alone, but I convinced her to wear her jacket and told myself to buy her some boots before the next visit.

Our tutoring sessions went well. She was easy to talk to when there were no outside distractions. We read several books and watched as many movies. The surprising thing to me was the rapport that began to develop between her and Muriel. I think it began with the first book I gave Brandi. According to her, Muriel had read the book and made a few comments to her.

"I was sittin' on my bed readin' *Emmeline* when Ol' Muriel came in. She says oh you're reading that book. A friend of mine knew about the people. I said yeah sure. She said Emmeline was considered crazy and a witch by the community. They never trusted her. I said whatever. The big question she said was would it really still be incest if neither Emmeline nor her son knew they were related. So I said well how could you not know something like that? She said she thought it was quite possible since the child was only half Emmeline. The other half was a stranger really. So how could Emmeline even begin to guess what her son would look like, how he would act, what kind of job he would have, or where he would live and all of this almost twenty years later?

"Well, we got into a big discussion about Emmeline that night. We talked about it for a long time. Then we started talking about growing up and families and stuff like that. Muriel told me she was orphaned as a little kid and grew up in a convent. I said it must of been nice--clean and quiet and somebody to wait on you all the time. She said it was clean and quiet, but nobody waited on her. She had to do a lot of chores after her homework and on weekends. She said the worst part was she had no friends. Kids came and left the convent so much that she would just start to make friends with a girl and the girl would leave. Only Muriel never left—not until she went away forever when she went to college. She went to the University and then did a whole lot of neat things. Before that her life wasn't all that great."

I started bringing three books whenever Brandi and I began a new novel. Muriel read the books with us, and we all talked about them. At first I was surprised by her insightful comments. Then I came to realize that Muriel was an intelligent woman, and I decided that both Brandi and I could learn something from her We met two or three times a week for over two months, until Brandi's case came before the judge for hearing. The school gave me release time to attend the court hearing; Brandi's parents sent word they would not be there.

4

On a chilly day in April, I walked into the County Courthouse to hear the judge's decision on the future of Brandi Robb. The only other person I noticed present there in the interest of Brandi was Muriel Buckman.   She looked quite a bit different dressed in street clothes, still heavy, but wearing a dark brown pant suit that minimized her bulk.   A brightly printed scarf knotted loosely around her neck brightened up the outfit.   I sat down next to her on a bench near the front of the room.

Brandi turned around in her seat at a table near the judge's bench. Noticing Muriel and me, she smiled and gave us two thumbs up.   Her hair was brushed into soft poufs around her head.   I noticed she was wearing a new outfit: gray pants and a navy blazer with a bright red jersey underneath.

On her feet were the black platform shoes.

During the time I had been tutoring her, she and Muriel had become friendly; then a bond seemed to develop between them. At first, I was surprised that the woman bothered with the girl.   After all, many adolescents came and went at the Youth Detention Center.   Didn't she see Brandi as just another rude, foul-mouthed, poorly dressed ruffian to be channeled through the judicial process, then sent on her way? Apparently not.   I guessed that both of us had been drawn to this girl because we sensed something special behind the facade: an intelligent, sensitive, and insightful young lady.   It wasn't until I got to know her better that I came to understand Muriel's attachment to Brandi.

When I first met Muriel Buckman, I asked around and learned enough to set my mind at ease that Brandi was in good hands while being held at the Center.   The more I learned about the woman, the more impressed I became.   A native of Houlton, Maine, Muriel was thirty-two years old, widowed, and childless.   An only child, her parents died when she was seven, at which time the only relative, an older uncle, sent her to a convent school in New York State.   She stayed there until graduation from high school, then entered the University of Maine on a scholarship, majoring in English and Criminal Justice.   After college, she joined the Department of Human Services, first as a caseworker, later leaving the office to become a special field services representative at the State Youth Detention Center. When the old uncle died, Muriel inherited a substantial portfolio of stocks, bonds, and real estate. She owned her own house on a lake in a small town outside of Portland. She had a long list of volunteer projects, all having to do with helping troubled teens. She was not a stereotypical "jail guard." Her presence at Brandi's hearing was not unusual for the woman, either, because she took exceptional interest in her charges.

A social worker from DHS, a court-appointed psychologist, and a public defender presented their reports to the court. Macy's had dropped the charges; apparently they had been convinced that it was in the public interest, and in their own, to do so. The judge leaned toward returning Brandi to the community and to the school system, provided a suitable living situation could be found for her. When asked for her recommendation, the social worker named Muriel, and the judge called her to the bench.

To my surprise, Muriel had offered to provide room and board and to serve as legal guardian. She never had done that much for one of her cases before. Brandi would live with Muriel, return to school, and finish the year in the eighth grade. The judge looked over a sheaf of papers in a large packet, nodding his head as he read. Then he asked Brandi if the arrangement was acceptable to her. "Oh, yeah, Judge, it's great."

The judge sentenced her to three months at the State Youth Detention Center, time already served by her incarceration prior to the hearing, then a six-month probation, after which all parties would return to court. At that time, the judge planned to assess Brandi's progress and decide how to proceed. Everyone agreed upon the arrangement.

After the judge left, I went out to the lobby to wait. Surprised as I was about Muriel, her decision to take Brandi under her wing impressed me. With her help, Brandi stood a good chance of making it out of the pit kids like her landed in though lousy circumstances.

Shortly, they emerged from the courtroom. Both of them were smiling.

"Yo, Ms. M. What's up? Muriel and I are celebrating and goin' to Old Country Buffet. Do you wanna go with us? Can she come, Mure?"

"That's a good idea," Muriel said. "We need to get some things worked out about school if you're going to start back on Monday."

"Yeah, well, you can do that later. I thought we'd go shopping after lunch, since we'll be at the Mall anyway." Brandi laughed.

"Very practical," said Muriel. "Well, then, what are we waiting for?"

5

I didn't hear very much about Brandi for most of the rest of the school year. Once in a while, one of the eighth grade teachers would mention something she did, but nothing warranted a suspension. She seemed to be readjusting to the school routine and adapting to life with Muriel.

Most eighth graders despised the last week of school. They couldn't wait to get out: they knew they were headed to the high school and refused to do any more work. The eighth grade teachers hated the last week of school, too. Grades had been finalized, the students often acted out of control, and the heat and the lack of air conditioning compounded the problem. Tank tops, crop tops, and muscle shirts appeared in such volume that it was impossible to send everyone to the office. The boys mostly wore long, loose shorts, but the girls tended to wear very brief, tight shorts. Sometimes they tried to get away with wearing sports bras and short, clingy lycra work-out tights.

On Wednesday we moved into the home-stretch, the last morning of the school year. Everyone was pretty excited. Yearbooks had been passed out early that morning, and the kids had spent the time until the final assembly looking at the pictures and signing each others' books. Then the Honors Assembly, an all-school affair held in the gym, started. The eighth graders received the big school awards, like highest academic average and citizenship awards; the seventh graders got certificates and pins for honor roll and community service, and the sixth graders watched, getting ideas about what awards they might receive the following year.

It was particularly hot that morning. All the doors to the gym were open, and some large fans blew air around, but the place was stifling. It was hot in the seating area on the floor, where the eighth graders, parents, and guests sat, but it was almost unbearable in the bleachers, especially near the top, where the sixth graders sat. In the past, Honors Assembly also was Dress-up Day, but dressing up had become less and less common in middle school, so most kids wore shorts and tee-shirts or tank tops. There weren't many female teachers in stockings or male teachers in jackets and ties, either. Quite a few wore shorts themselves.

I was sitting with my seventh grade class near the door to the corridor, in the first row of bleachers. One of the huge blue fans had been set up just outside the door, blowing warm air on us, and we leaned into its current, taking full advantage of the little bit of relief it provided. Most of my students fidgeted from boredom after the first fifteen or twenty minutes and showed more interest in jockeying for a position in front of the fan's breeze than in listening to the band, the chorus, and the speeches given by teachers and coaches presenting awards.

Since many of my former students received some of the awards, I listened to parts of the assembly, trying to catch their names. I knew who was getting what award and tuned out with the kids, paying attention only when the award being announced was for one of my students from the year before. Brandi had made a few mistakes since her return from the Detention Center, but her overall behavior was so much better that even Mrs. Hough, the most skeptical of her teachers, was impressed. She earned nothing lower than a B-, which meant she made the honor roll for the fourth quarter. The teachers put Brandi's name on the list of students to be honored for improvement over the course of the year. All awards were supposed to be a surprise, but parents were notified ahead of time and invited, so the kids knew they were getting some kind of award if they saw a parent in the audience. Muriel was seated with the guests on the end of the third row

The gym got noisier as the program dragged on. People became uncomfortable, distracted, and impatient. I was lulled into a sort of half-sleep by the whirring of the fan, and the various noises in the room had melded into a single droning sound. A change in the tone jerked me out of my stupor. There was some kind of commotion off to my right about halfway between the bleachers and the stage. I caught a glimpse of a tall, dark-haired boy, in long shorts and a tee shirt, who appeared to be yelling, but I couldn't hear any words over the growing noise of raised voices. About three years had passed since I had taught this boy in my class, but I recognized Dean Muzzio and immediately tasted bile rising from my stomach into my throat. Of the many students I've known over the years, Dean was the only one whose threats I took seriously.

6

Everything about Dean appeared normal except his eyes. A tall sixteen-year-old, he was slender and good-looking, in a dark, Mediterranean way. His father was tall and swarthy, and Dean took after him in looks: tawny skin, prominent nose, curly black hair, and opaque brown eyes, deep and luminous like mud puddles. He followed his father's lead in other ways, as well. A fierce temper led him to threaten people when he was angry and to resort to fist fighting when he lost control. Both Muzzios were abusers of weaker and smaller people, especially females who in some way were vulnerable. The dead give-away was the eyes. They went flat, hard and shiny, moments before any last vestige of restraint failed and the frustration erupted into physical confrontation. I had heard stories about Mr. Muzzio and had experienced his son's fury once, three years before.

At that time my students had been arranged around tables, reading paperback novels together. Dean was seated beside his one friend in my class, Darren, a blond-haired boy of medium build and quiet demeanor. Two girls sat at their table, both of them good students academically and popular with their classmates. Jenny was a petite redhead and a chatterbox; Melanie was taller, with short, light brown hair, easy-going and comfortable around most people.

Moving around the room to check the progress of each group, I paused at Dean's table. "How's everything going here?" I addressed them.

"Okay, I guess," answered Melanie.

"Only okay?" I asked.

"Well, sort of," Jenny said, looking toward Darren.

"It's a hard book," Darren spoke up but didn't look at me.

"It's not that hard—you've read harder ones before."

"Well, it's easier keeping a journal than discussing it," said Jenny.

"Why is that, do you think?" I asked.

Nobody answered at first. Then Dean leaned his chair back, balancing it on two legs with the back against the wall. Propping his head against the blackboard behind him, arms stretched in front and gripping the table, he looked at me and said, "Reading sucks. I'm sick of it." The other three students lowered their heads.

"Look, Dean, I know it's hard sometimes, but, if you put your mind to it, you can do fine. And working in a group should make the task more fun"

I knew he read poorly, so I deliberately had made up the group to include Jenny and Melanie because they were good readers, hard workers, and got along with everyone.

"Yeah, well this stinks, and I'm not doing this shit anymore." By now the entire class had stopped reading, and the room was silent the way it never was normally.

"Dean, we can talk about this later. Let's just finish up the period in our groups."

"I don't like people getting in my way. When they do, I get a little crazy." Dean's hands clenched the edge of the table, and, when I looked into his eyes, they stared at me, hard and flat. He continued, "If I get crazy, I start breaking heads."

I've been sworn at and threatened by students several times over the course of my teaching career, but I never had considered a threat serious before. Looking at Dean's tense body, the muscles in his arms taut, the mouth drawn tight, and the eyes riveted on mine, I believed this boy was serious.

"Are you threatening us?"

"I'm feeling a little crazy, and they're in my way." He gestured with his chin toward the two girls sitting across the table, between him and me. "You're in my way, too." I visualized the table going over on the girls if Dean decided to flip it and come after me.

Feeling the whole class waiting to see what I would do, I unlocked my eyes from Dean's, moved back a step or two, and spoke quietly to Jenny and Melanie. "Go get your journals and take some notes on the chapter." When they moved quickly from their seats, I looked toward Darren, avoiding Dean's glare, and said, "Why don't you two guys take a walk to the art room and on the way figure out what supplies you want for the book project."

Darren rose immediately, mumbled, "Com'on, Dean," and headed out of the room. I watched as Dean followed Darren into the corridor. After they left, the room buzzed with unleashed tension.

One boy asked if I was okay. "That Dean's a bad dude," he said.

"Please get him out of our class," Jenny spoke, her eyes bright with tears. "He's nasty, Ms. M." One day, I thought, that boy was going to hurt someone.

Now it looked like that day had come.

7

About the same moment I recognized Dean at the Honors Assembly, I became aware of three things in rapid succession. He was swinging a gun around, students were scrambling away, and Brandi was moving from her seat near the foot of the stage. She ran right at him, shouting something, I thought, and he seemed to be shouting back. I saw her throw herself at him and then heard the unmistakable sound of a gun going off. They both went down about the time that my view was blocked by a mass of people. The volume of the noise grew, as people screamed, running toward exits, scraping chairs on the floor, and ducking under the bleachers.

Piecing together information from Muriel and from some of the staff who were closer to the scene, I was able to recreate what happened the morning that changed several people's lives. Dean had walked into the gym through the outer doorway that led from the parking lot. His height set him apart from most of the students, and the majority of people recognized him, either from an unpleasant encounter or by his reputation The scowl on his face kept most at a distance, but John McIntyre, the instructor in the school's mechanics shop, said hello to Dean, as he moved to the wall inside the second set of doors.

"Howyadoin'", Dean said. He shifted his position and pressed his back against the wall. John gave Dean a once-over look, nodded, and moved away to join the group of students he was responsible for watching.

Dean waited on the periphery a few more minutes. No one else came up to him; no one else spoke to him. He pulled away from the wall and walked toward the front of the gym. Nobody noticed anything wrong until Dean started yelling obscenities. Then people looked in his direction, not yet concerned. When he pulled a gun from his pocket, a couple of students standing close by screamed. No teacher was in the vicinity, and Dean started to run toward the stage.

He said, "You're all to blame," and waved the gun over his head.

Brandi, sitting about ten rows away, advanced, shouting something like, "You jerk, Dean. Don't ruin this, asshole."

Dean must have become a little confused because he hesitated for an instant. Just as he raised the gun, Brandi reached him and lunged, setting him off balance. They both started to fall, and then the gun went off. In that moment, a couple of people close by were able to grab Dean, and more people moved to disarm him and pin him down.

"Get off me, damn you. Brandi. Are you all right? Brandi. Let me go. I need to help her."

Brandi lay face-down on the floor, her hair fanned out around her head, her foot touching a crumpled potato chip bag someone had tossed away. One arm was down at her side; the other stretched over her head, and the book she had been holding lay open just beyond her curved fingers. A cacophony of noise - strident, discordant, meaningless - filled the gym, yet it was quiet around Brandi's prone body. She was surrounded by a stillness that rendered the yelling meaningless. Dean wrestled himself from the grip of his captors and moved to Brandi, kneeling by her head. He touched her cheek with his fingertips; the contrast between his dark skin and her pale complexion emphasized her whiteness. She made no response, and Dean moaned. "Oh, what have I done? Brandi, wake up. Please. I didn't mean to hurt you. Please, Brandi. Look at me."

Brandi's eyes remained closed. Her face, soft and pallid, contrasted with the scuffed brown floor under her. Several people grasped Dean's arms and pulled him upright. They whisked him from the scene, his curses and screams rising above the racket made by the crowd. At the door, two policemen moved in to take Dean, and, as he was hustled from the gym into a cruiser, his howls rose in volume, the last sound before the cruiser's door closed coming out as a strangled version of her name: "Braaa nnn d." The car door slammed, the siren wound up to add to the noise, and Dean disappeared from the scene.

While all the commotion was going on with Dean, Brandi lay on the gym floor. The noise and the people swirled around her, but her body remained quiet. Finally, the team from the local rescue unit arrived, and eventually they put her on a stretcher and carried her to the van. It, too, disappeared from the scene, lights flashing and horn blasting.

Sitting with my husband in the waiting room of City Medical Center that June evening after the tragedy, I wondered why Brandi had thrown her life into the fray, but I couldn't answer myself, not then. My body felt numb; I didn't feel the edges of the orange plastic chair, even though I could see that there was a long crack running its length and a piece of the bottom edge broken off. An overhead pager buzzed frequently, and names were called out of its square black shape, hung from the wall like a pennant strung-up a halyard and flapping meaningless sounds into the void.

Muriel came over and sat next to me; we talked quietly. I learned that Dean was one of Brandi's old buddies from the days of her suspension. In fact, he had been with her at the mall the day she got caught shoplifting. Also, he was one of the boys who supplied the others with pills, as well as alcohol.

I looked at the people who had come to check on Brandi's condition. Besides Muriel and me, there were an eighth grade teacher, a couple of administrators, and even a few students. When the doctor entered the room, Muriel's body jerked. Everyone stopped chatting and craned necks or leaned in their direction in order to hear.

The doctor was a little guy, about half the size of Muriel. He had light skin, light hair in a short brush cut, and wore green scrubs that were wrinkled and stained with what appeared to me to be blood. Looking exhausted, with a pinched mouth and sunken eyes further depressed by the thick lenses of steel-rimmed glasses that lay slightly askew on his nose, he spoke tentatively. "Ms. Buckman?"

Muriel rose, moved toward him, and asked, "Is she going to live?"

"She should pull through." He spoke softly, so I barely could hear.

"It's still touch and go. A gun-shot wound at close range is very dangerous, and the operation was difficult. We're worried because she lost a lot of blood, and she's not out of danger yet. But we're optimistic she will recover completely in time."

"Can I see her?" Muriel asked.

"Only for a couple of minutes and only from the doorway. She isn't conscious yet, and she's very weak." Muriel motioned for me to go along with her. The doctor started to say something, but she shot him a look, and he stopped. We followed him through the doorway of the waiting room, down the hall, and into the ICU, stopping at the door to one room where two nurses were adjusting machines and writing on charts.

The body in the bed did not resemble Brandi. It looked smaller, dwarfed by the machines. Tubes ran from one of the machines and from a bag hanging on a rolling rack to her nose, arm, and under the sheet in the vicinity of her abdomen. She was wearing a light blue hospital gown with a white sheet drawn to just above her stomach. Usually her color was high: rosy cheeks and an all-over pinkish glow. Against the stark shades of the hospital room, her face was dull white, tinged with a sickly green cast. If the doctor hadn't said she would live, I'd have thought she was on her deathbed.

We stood watching for a few minutes, then left. When we returned to the waiting room, most of the others had gone. At the far end of the room, my husband lounged in a lurid orange, plastic-like upholstered couch--it made me think of a wet pumpkin skin--and rose as we approached. Muriel waved a hand, dropped to a matching chair set perpendicular to the couch, and I sat next to my husband. "How do things look?" he asked.

I didn't want to say how bad I thought Brandi looked, but before I could think of something to say that would not cause Muriel to lose any hope she might have, she answered, "It's wait and see, I guess, just like most of life is. It's tough. You do things, stupid things, terrible things, and somehow you survive in spite of your own mistakes. But when you do things right, sometimes it's not enough. Life just goes along the way it's going to, and you can't control it."

Neither my husband nor I said anything. I was trying to think of a half-way intelligent response when Muriel continued. "I did some things when I was a teenager that I've wished I could change. I go back over and over the past. If willing your life to be different depended on how hard you wished, the mess I made of everything when I was a kid would have been deleted like someone--God maybe--took some White-out and just obliterated all the bad spots. But it just doesn't happen like that. I finally thought He'd forgiven me--or I'd forgiven myself--when Brandi came along."

I wasn't sure how to respond to Muriel. I wasn't sure she wanted any response. I wasn't even sure she was talking to us.

"I hated the school. The staff were good enough to me, but I never had any friends--nobody stayed there very long. Just me. It was so lonely."

There was a long pause. Then, "It wasn't a convent, the way some people thought. I never bothered to correct them--it didn't seem important. It was a Christian school. Either way, they'd have done the same thing. In the end it didn't matter. "

"Muriel, are you all right?" I finally asked. I wanted to be sure she realized where she was and if she meant to be talking to us.

"Yes, I'm all right. No, I'm not all right. I'd just like to sit here and talk. I feel like sifting through the stuff that's caught in my head, see if I can get some of it sorted out. And if you don't mind hanging around, I wish you would stay here with me so it doesn't look like I'm just talking to myself."

"Okay, that's fine," I said. "We won't be able to sleep, anyway, and I don't want to leave you alone." I thought that a hospital is the ideal place to lay out the pieces of your life, try to put together what's blown apart. Nobody expects anyone to be rational or in control in the waiting area of a hospital emergency room. Everything is out of control, anyway.

We looked pretty normal, considering the other folks around us. In the far corner of the room, a couple now sat, his big body shaking from the effect of deep, although nearly silent, sobbing. The shaking caused a tattoo on his right biceps to move in a jerky rhythm. I watched the tattoo for a minute or so, then focused on the man's grubby blue tank top. It was nearly the same color as his partner's dress, though the clothing and the whole demeanor of the woman were neater, cleaner, kind of crisp and quiet, I thought without really putting any effort into the observation. New visitors briefly caught my attention. A few young people, early twenties probably, burst into the room, squabbling, bloody, loud. A nurse followed soon after, asked them to lower their voices, and left. I felt suspended in the crazy-quilt patchwork of the hospital at night, where, amid a kind of surreal atmosphere, hard facts, like accidents, disease, fights, bring death to life for real. "What did they do to you at the school?"

"They didn't do it. It just got harder and harder to be alone. The day kids, the ones who lived around the place and came there just for school, didn't pay any attention to me. They had their own house and family, friends, jobs, things to do. I was a fat nobody who took up one seat in the classroom. Sometimes I'd make up stories about being one of the townies. I gave myself another name and a big family--parents, grandparents who lived with us, lots of brothers and sisters. I'd lie in bed at night building the house.

When it was done, I renovated and redecorated it so many times it became probably three or four different houses. I did the same thing with the family. Sometimes my parents were Irish, sometimes German, or just American, Italian, Swiss, blond, dark, redheaded. Three brothers and three sisters, four and two, two and four. Grandparents who loved us all, cooked special foods for birthdays, told us family secrets, spent lots of time with each grandchild. It kept me going for so long. But finally it wasn't enough anymore." Muriel spoke hardly above a whisper; I had to strain sometimes to hear her above the commotions coming and going in the room. She sat with her upper body slumped over her knees, head propped in her hands.

"What happened?" my husband asked. His voice was very soft, just as low as Muriel's. She continued speaking in the same quiet, controlled tone.

"Terry came along the summer I was sixteen. He was the handyman for the place--did all the things the staff couldn't do or didn't have time for-- yard work, fixing things around the buildings, running errands or driving people places they needed to go. That's how I got to know him. That summer I had problems with my teeth and had to go to the dentist a lot. Terry drove me. The dentist's office was almost an hour from the school. So we had a lot of time alone together.

"At first we didn't say much. But he was the kind of person who talked to everybody, and pretty soon we were talking about all kinds of things. He was the first person who ever really took an interest in what I thought or how I felt. Terry was kind, and I believed--I still believe--he was sincere. They drove him away."

Muriel stopped talking, so I cut in. "Why did they make him go away?"

"You already know the answer. It's the oldest story in the book." She laughed a little, but I saw the tears framing her eyes. "Yeah, I got pregnant. The predictable outcome for a homely, lonely girl who suddenly is befriended and dazzled by a good-looking, worldly, older boy. I've seen it so many times in the last fifteen years, and it's so obvious. But it wasn't obvious to me, and I will never believe Terry would have deserted me if they hadn't forced him to go. He was in college and poor--he wouldn't have been working at that school unless he badly needed the money. They threatened him, I know."

"Threatened him about what?"

"Statutory rape. It wasn't rape, but I wasn't eighteen, and they were appalled that their mousy home girl, who'd been there so long they considered me a piece of furniture, could possibly muster the initiative to participate in an act of love. So they decided it was rape, sent Terry packing, and hid me away in the back rooms where nobody could see me. I was so ashamed."

"Oh, Muriel," I whispered, reaching my arm awkwardly toward her. "Did they make you have an abortion?"

She stretched in the chair, touching my fingers as she did so, then put her head back and closed her eyes. She didn't say anything for a while. I took a breath, sat, and waited. Presently, Muriel continued, "I sometimes think an abortion would have been better--easier for me to deal with, anyway. I thought about it when I first thought Terry had deserted me because I was pregnant. After I realized that they made him leave, I wanted to have the baby because it was part of Terry. They said it was right for me to have the baby." Muriel sniffed. "I wanted to have the baby, and they wanted me to have the baby but not for the same reasons. It was too late to do anything when I finally realized their plan."

"Their plan? What was their plan?"

"They had decided to give the baby away, have her or him--I don't even know whether it was a boy or a girl--adopted by a good Christian family. I pleaded with them, but they had all the power. They told me I couldn't raise a baby because I was a ward of the State, I had no resources, I had no high school diploma, I had nothing. A family could give the baby all the opportunities I never had. Oh, you know, they used all the arguments that are still used. And I could see no way out; they were right. Terry was gone. I didn't have anybody to turn to for advice. I was so lonely. So finally I signed the papers--they said they could have them signed for me because I was a juvenile and in their custody, but it was better if I did it myself. I signed away my baby's life to strangers forever. It was the worst thing I ever did. Making a baby with Terry was not evil, but giving up that baby was."

She was sobbing now. While I was trying to think what to say, my husband spoke. "You know in your heart what you did wasn't evil. You were a scared kid, and you got tough advice. You weren't given any options. Have you tried to find your child now that he's an adult?"

"The records were lost. Maybe deliberately, maybe not. But I can't find anything anywhere. I signed away any rights I had, and they managed somehow to destroy the paperwork. The adoption was private. I think it probably wasn't even legal. But there's nothing to go on. Believe me, I've tried. I searched; I hired both a lawyer and an investigator.

They couldn't find anything."

"I'm so sorry."

"Well, yes, it was a sorry situation. I mourned that loss for years. That's one of the reasons why I started to help other kids in trouble whenever I could. I think I was so attracted to Brandi because I saw some of myself in her. Oh, not the brashness--I never acted like that. I was too scared. But the vulnerability under her know-it-all veneer. That was the same. I guess maybe, too, I see her as a second chance for me. She's become the child I gave away. I've finally got her back after all the empty years--and now I might lose her. Life really isn't fair. I know that, but it's still not right. It's just too unfair."

"We don't know anything for certain yet," my husband responded. "There's no sense assuming too much. Brandi's in good hands. Probably the best thing you can do for her and for yourself is go home and try to sleep a little. If she's better tomorrow, she's going to need you, and you're going to need your strength no matter what."

I thought my husband was being rather curt and dismissive, especially after all Muriel had shared with us, but apparently that was what she wanted. At any rate, she stood up and seemed to gain strength just doing so. "Yes, that's a good idea. You know, I've never told that to anybody before. It feels good to tell you. Now you know a little secret of mine--that feels good too. Thanks for staying here."

We hugged a long time in that ugly orange room. Then we walked to the parking lot and hugged some more before getting into our cars and leaving.

On the ride home, we talked a little about what Muriel had told us about her life. Then I expressed my anger at how unfair it seemed that this tragedy should happen to Brandi now that her life finally had taken a turn for the better.

"You're right. But what about Dean? Seems like he could use a break, too," my husband commented.

"What do you mean? He's the one who went haywire and threatened all of us," I reacted indignantly.

"Obviously, he's at the end of his rope. You told me he's failing school again. Plus his father is suspected of abusing him, even though the kid denies it. And then maybe having to work with the guy? I think he's begging for help," he said.

"Well, that was a lousy way to do it."

"Yes, but maybe it's the only way he could think of. He must feel so alone, and he's desperate for someone to notice. If he denied any physical abuse by his father, the authorities can't do anything. If Dean won't go that route for help, nobody can step in and take him from the home." I didn't respond then, but in the weeks ahead, I thought about my husband's words and realized that somebody should intervene in Dean's home life before we all paid for his father's abusive ways.

<h1 style="text-align:center">8</h1>

I didn't see Brandi again until mid-August, when Muriel invited my husband and me to her house on a Saturday afternoon. She had taken a leave of absence from the Youth Detention Center so that she could be with Brandi all of the time.

The weather was wonderful: sunny, dry air, temperature about eighty degrees. Her small, cedar log house was unpretentious, but the setting was spectacular: a narrow, deep, heavily wooded lot that ended at the shore of the lake, with a stunning view west toward the distant White Mountains. Boaters, jet skiers, canoers, and fisherman in small motorboats crisscrossed the water.

Wooden boxes filled with pink geraniums adorned all the windows across the front of the house, and pots of other bright-colored flowers stood on a deck that stretched across the back of the house. On the deck were a gas grill, a round, glass-topped table and four green-cushioned chairs, and two green striped chaise lounges. In one of the lounges sat a slimmer, deeply tanned, blond-haired Brandi. Barefoot, she wore white shorts and a yellow tank top. Through a gap between the waistband of the shorts and the bottom of the shirt I could see a thick, reddish scar running vertically along her abdomen.

"Yo, Ms. M., how's it going? Hi, Mr. M. Sorry, I can't get up. I don't move very fast yet. Once I get comfortable in the chair, I'm supposed to stay put. I do my therapy stuff in the morning and veg out in the afternoon. Ya caught me veggin' out. It's good for getting a great tan, though, huh. My hair got bleached out with all the sun. Do ya like it? I helped it with some peroxide. Muriel went out to the store to get some stuff for supper. We're--she's--gonna barbecue. She's a great cook. She'll be back in a few minutes. Com'on and sit down and clue me in on what's been happenin'."

Brandi talked non-stop, grinning and gesticulating constantly, but she did not move around much. After we told her about our summer and I shared what I knew of the people she asked about, she began to tell us about the Honors Assembly on the last day of school.

"I knew I was gonna get the Improvement award before I saw Muriel in the audience. I mean, it doesn't take a genius type to figure out what teachers like and all. Even Mrs. Hough probably voted for me. She was so relieved that I wasn't on her case when I came back from the Center, she would have done just about anything to keep me from screwin' around. I know she gave me a B- just cuz she was glad to be rid of me. She woulda died if I came back again for eighth grade. Ha! That woulda killed her." Brandi laughed.

"Anyway, I wasn't surprised. But you know what did surprise me? I was happy about the award. I always used to shit on those dumb awards and the jerks who thought they were so cool. I figured they didn't know anything. But they've been on to somethin' pretty good. It was me who didn't know nothing. Funny, it's so hard being a tough bitchin' woman--on the streets, with the guys, keepin' up the image. Ha, it was a cinch just getting B's and kissin' up to teachers and stuff. And it blew me away that I was feelin' good about it that morning.

"Then I saw Dean come in the gym. I knew he was gonna start trouble. I'd seen him the day before--when he found out he flunked tenth grade, again--and he was royally pissed. I've seen him pissed before, but this was more than usual. He had his sixteenth birthday, and his dad--boy, there's a sommabitch if there ever was one--told him he'd have to quit and come to work for him if he didn't pass this year. Called him a dumb f. You know what I mean."

"I can guess," I answered.

"His dad has a shop at his house--he fixes cars and stuff. Dean hates it, and he hates his dad. The asshole is a big bully--he beats up on him. He's been doing it since Dean was a little kid. He couldn't fight back then. He tries now, but he still can't beat his old man. The creep works out, liftin' weights and stuff, just so he can take on Dean. That kinda guy oughtta not live."

Remembering an encounter I had with Mr. Muzzio when Dean was a student, I recalled the man's anger and his physical power.

"Anyway, "Brandi continued, "He was in an evil way on Tuesday, cursing everybody, even his old teachers at the middle school. He was out to hurt somebody--he wanted to hurt his father, but he couldn't."

I glanced at my husband, who gave me one of his "I told you so" looks.

I rolled my eyes and turned back to Brandi.

"He started talkin' crazy--said he wanted to get even with school and the teachers. Since the high school was finished for the year, he couldn't get anybody there. I told him to forget it. Maybe he could go to summer school and make up the classes, but he said he'd tried that last year and it didn't work. The teachers in summer school were the worst assholes. I told him to chill out, but he was still pretty ripped when some of his buddies picked him up. They left to go drinkin'--when Dean drinks, he gets real ugly.

"So, when I saw him in the gym, I knew it was gonna be a bad scene. I didn't see the gun at first. I thought he was just gonna pull a horror show--scream, cuss, gross people out, like that. Then I saw the gun, and I sorta went nuts. I don't know-- I guess I've started likin' being a rube and a geek--that's what Dean called me Tuesday. And I really like livin' with Muriel--she's one cool lady. I mean, who'd mind livin' in this place? It's a castle compared to the dumps I've been in. She's not a pushover, though--don't think that-- she's tough. But she's fair. And if I do stuff right, she really puts out. She doesn't just pay me off--actually she doesn't give me money. I 'have to earn it.' But we do stuff--go places and see things and stuff like that. Maybe it sounds stupid, but I have fun with her. And I don't wanna go back to what it was like."

"It doesn't sound stupid to me at all," I said. "It sounds really nice."

"Anyway, I kinda lost my cool. I saw Dean screwin' up bad. I was afraid he'd screw it up for me, too. I wanted to stop him before he really blew it. Muriel told me he could get some help if he wanted it. Not from her--she said she isn't a 'masochist'--ha, ha-- but there were places and people who would help him. But that scene with the gun in the gym--I was afraid he'd lose any chance to be helped. And his father probably really would kill him after that. I figured he would listen to me. I didn't think about the gun. I never thought he'd fire it at me--I still don't think he did, either. I think it was an accident. But, shit, nobody gives a care about him now. And if they try him as an adult and he goes to Wardham, forget it, man. He'll come out so evil, he really will kill somebody."

Brandi leaned back in the lounge and closed her eyes. Under the tan, her face seemed a little drawn. "Are you getting tired?" I asked.

"Yeah, kinda. But that's okay. I can sleep after you leave. You're my first visitors this summer except for a few of the kids from school—and they could only stay an hour at a time before Muriel told them to leave and 'come back again for another short visit.' Jeez, she's a real mother-hen," she laughed.

"Why don't you take a nap now? I'll help Muriel when she gets back, and we can talk some more later."

"Okay, as long as you promise not to go. If you want you can read my journal. You can, too, Mr. M.--you don't have to, though--it's probably boring to you. But Ms. M. likes boring teacher stuff, like journals. Ha. That's one thing I've been able to do all summer. It might bore even you this time, though, cuz it's so long."

Muriel arrived a few minutes later, laden with brown grocery bags. I helped her by putting away some of the things, and she got Brandi's journal.

This one was a plain red-covered loose-leaf notebook full of lined paper, much of it filled with her handwriting. I found the place where, when she was recovering in the hospital, she'd started writing about her injuries and began to read:

"I guess I almost died. Its funny cuz so many times in my life I wished I was dead. I must of wanted to live real bad this time cuz the doctor said I had a 'strong will to live'--those were his words. So I guess when it came down to livin or diein', I really wanted to live. I don't remember being afraid or thinking about whether I wanted to live or die or anything. Its pretty hazy when I try to think about it. The bullet hit me in the belly and made a mess inside. There was a lotta blood. I lost so much they thought I was gonna die. In the rescue truck, they were yellin and stuff--I remember a little--I herd the siren--then

I don't remember more till after I was at City Med."

Thinking about the time Brandi tried to hang herself and her other suicidal activities, I admired her will and stamina in the face of such a tremendous physical threat. I flipped some pages in the notebook and started reading another entry:

"I feel sorry for Dean. I know he didnt meen to shoot me but nobody else believes it and they dont care anyway. He was in the county jail, but I think he's been moved to the Youth Center. I dont know whats gonna happen. I cant visit him cuz I cant go very far in a car yet. But as soon as I can. Im gonna go see him and tell him I dont blame him. I wrote him a letter--two acktully--but he didnt write back."

"I go to the hospital once a week for a check-up and for therapy. I guess the bullet tore up some organs and stuff and did somethin' to a nurve too. I need therapy for my leg. Its pretty stiff and hurts to walk. Thats gonna take a while. But I should be okay by school. I hope so anyway. It's funny, I never thought Id think so, but I really wanna start high school.

I looked at my husband and said, "This is an incredible change in so short a time."

PART THREE

1

Brandi began her first year of high school a few weeks later, but, still being quite weak, she attended only the morning classes. Muriel returned to the Youth Detention Center on a part time basis.

In order to help her keep up with assignments, I continued tutoring Brandi, driving twice a week to the lake house. Sometimes Muriel asked me to stay for supper, and, when my husband was away on business, I generally did, welcoming the delicious cooking and the equally good company.

All during the fall Brandi tried to convince Muriel to let her visit Dean. He had been moved from the county jail to the Youth Detention Center until his case came up for a hearing on the court schedule. Muriel was dead-set against any interaction between the kids, and Brandi worked on eliciting my support each time I was there. Muriel wasn't above trying to get me to side with her, either. Even though I privately agreed with Muriel's feelings about keeping Dean as far away from Brandi as possible, I did my best to stay out of the discussion, wanting to remain on good terms with both of them. Attempting to win her case by the sheer repetition of her pleas and by wearing down Muriel, Brandi never let up.

Finally, the court assigned Dean's case a hearing date for mid-October.

As a compromise for refusing to allow her to visit him, Muriel offered to take Brandi to the proceedings at Superior Court, and she jumped at the opportunity. Because I had been asked to represent the school, I planned to attend the hearing, also, although I didn't look forward to the experience.

"I just want to say hi to him for a couple of minutes. Nothin's gonna happen, Mure. Com'on, give me a break." Brandi was whining at Muriel when I approached the front of the doors to the courtroom on the day of the hearing.

"All right," Muriel responded, "but take it easy, okay?"

"Sure I will," Patting her on the shoulder, Brandi waved a hand in my direction and walked down the corridor toward a bench where Dean sat alongside a gray-haired man in a suit. I recognized the face from T.V. ads: Scott Louden, a well-known defense attorney with the reputation for taking impossible cases and getting his client off.

"Who's paying for that guy?" I asked Muriel in lieu of a greeting.

"Good question," she said. "I can't imagine who'd put up the kind of money he demands for Dean. I think his father's all but disowned him at this point, and his mother is a weakling. I don't think they can possibly have that kind of money unless someone is helping out, though I can't imagine why."

"Brandi looks good," I said, to change the subject. "She only limps a little now."

"She's coming along fine. We still need to keep up the weekly physical therapy, though. It's a slow process and will take a while."

Brandi looked very nice in a dress. From the expression on his face, Dean obviously thought so, too. Probably he'd never seen her in a dress. That fall she'd taken an interest in sprucing up and had used her school money, as well as some extra from Muriel, to buy a few skirts and a couple of dresses.

Although I couldn't hear anything the two kids said, the hug they exchanged resounded loud and clear for anybody to hear. Definitely there was a strong bond between them, and I sensed, rather than saw, a disapproving wince from Muriel.

If looks were any indication, Dean was a changed young man. Clean-shaven, with an expensive-looking haircut, he stood tall and straight in a blazer and slacks that fit him perfectly. The total effect was astounding. Gone were the baggy, rumpled pants, the soiled tee shirt, the scraggly hair, the stubbly face, the sneer that had hardly ever left his face. This young man looked as if he came from a fine prep school rather than a detention center. Impressed, I wondered again who was providing the money.

As we both watched Dean put his arm around Brandi while the two of them talked to Scott Louden. Muriel said, "I don't wish that boy any more grief than already's been thrown at him. We all know he's handled more hard knocks than anyone should get. But I'm worried about Brandi. I don't want her getting so close with him. I want the best of everything for her, and, regardless of the outward appearance, that boy is still Dean Muzzio inside."

Silently, I agreed with her. Probably it was uncharitable, but, at that moment, I still couldn't see beyond the meanness in the kid who had threatened my students and me. We turned to go into the courtroom just as Brandi, Dean, and Mr. Louden walked in our direction. Muriel continued inside to find seats, but I stopped and waited for the three of them, deciding I owed Dean a few words of encouragement. Paradoxically, I also felt a pang of anxiety for him as I remembered what my husband had said about the need for people to care about Dean.   In spite of my bad memories, I hoped things might go his way for once. "Hello, Dean. How are you?" I asked.

"Hi, Ms. M. Thanks for coming." He reached out and shook my hand, another astounding action, I thought.   I noticed that he used Brandi's name for me; I wanted to be miffed, but, since other students called me "Ms. M." also, I hardly could fault Dean.   I chalked up my uncharitable feelings toward him as left-over resentment from our past run-in with each other. I vowed to try and act less mean-spirited toward him.   The lawyer nodded to me, and we all entered the courtroom, but not before Brandi reached up on tiptoe and kissed Dean lightly on the cheek.

Later, I mused over the proceedings of the court hearing. Against all odds, or so I had thought back in June and throughout the summer, the judge determined that Dean would be tried in juvenile court rather than as an adult.   He must have seen something salvageable in the boy, some sign that more lenient treatment would be beneficial in the long run.

Of course, that high-priced lawyer might have helped the cause. He was a smooth talker and argued poignantly on Dean's behalf, alleging that "a bigger crime will be committed if the people send this boy, who made a mistake, to prison where hardened criminals, who like what they do, will teach him to become one of them, a menace to society.   This boy erred, yes; but let us not compound the error by refusing to offer the help he seeks, the help he needs, so that he can grow into a man and take his rightfulplace as a contributing member of our society."

On and on, Scott Louden expounded on the possibilities that might become reality if Dean were given this one chance. What a pompous windbag, I thought.   Always making reference to "the boy" and "the child," never even once calling him a young man, Louden showed great facility with words, though.   When he finished, even I believed in Dean, I, who knew the other side of this kid, the side the judge couldn't see under those clothes, that haircut, and his polite responses to questions. Now I wanted him to get that second chance, too.

The big surprise during the hearing was Brandi's testimony. When Scott Louden asked the judge to hear what the victim of the shooting had to say, I looked at Muriel and whispered, "Did you know she was going to speak here?"

By the look of shock on her face and the pallor of her skin, I knew the answer before Muriel mumbled, "No."

Looking like an innocent young lady in her pastel dress, Brandi charmed the judge with her straight talk. "Look, your Honor, Sir, hey, it was an accident. Dean would never shoot me on purpose. We're tight. I ran into him, and the gun went off. He never meant to shoot anybody. Did you know his father beats him up all the time? Sometimes he can't see for days cuz his father has beat on his head so bad that his eyes swole shut."

She went on about the abuses he had suffered, mostly at the hands of his father, a little bit about the things that happened to him at school, deflecting the attention from Dean's crime to his victimization. The judge listened intently to Brandi. I'm not sure, but I think that perhaps she was more responsible than Scott Louden for persuading the judge. Possibly someone might have saved a bundle of money on the expensive lawyer and just let Brandi handle the situation.

She was ecstatic over the decision. Dean would be confined at the Youth Center rather than in Wardham Prison. As a former "graduate" of the Center, Brandi knew that one could manage quite well there. Even if he were sentenced to stay there until he turned twenty-one, which was unlikely, he would have a relatively easy time of it compared to even a year at Wardham.

In the relatively short span of time between her incarceration at the Detention Center and Dean's, the public outcry as a result of newspaper articles on its sorry condition had focused attention on the Center and precipitated some positive changes. Most people thought that the Center reflected on the state in a shameful way. They were particularly troubled by the revelation of a "time-out" restraint chair. The proud citizens of Maine invested millions in luring tourists to the state but treated kids barbarically was the implicit message in the national press. People seemed embarrassed by the publicity and clamored for change.

It would take time to redress the situation completely, of course, but the Governor had begun by removing the administrative duties of the Youth Center from the Corrections Department to a task force he set up personally and made answerable only to him. Funds that had been denied for years began pouring into the place. The physical plant received attention first, since it had deteriorated so badly. The "time-out" chair was eliminated. Although an inmate of the Center still could expect to receive only a modicum of special tutoring, regular counseling, or comprehensive training projects, changes in those areas were in the making. However, none of these services would be available in the foreseeable future to Dean, or anyone else, doing time at the prison.

A more open atmosphere prevailed at the Youth Center. Not only a teacher paid by her school system, as I had been in Brandi's case, might visit; now family, friends, and other visitors also might come and go on a fairly open basis. There still would be checks of the people, but the administration was more attentive to the needs of the kids and to helping them. The previous Christmas, for instance, people provided a turkey dinner with all the trimmings, and, for the first time in memory, all of the kids confined at the Center got to sit down together to share the meal.

As far as Brandi was concerned, the changes translated into one thing: "This is great," she told me. "I can see Dean every day. We can chill together as much as we want."

2

Brandi didn't see Dean every day, but she managed to visit him at least once a week. Muriel argued with her initially, but in the end she gave into the entreaties. "Since we go right by there on the way to physical therapy, it's easy to just stop on the way home. I don't have to stay long, just enough to say hi and stuff." Muriel agreed it was "no hassle," as Brandi emphasized.

That much accomplished, as she shared with me during one of our tutoring sessions, Brandi proceeded to figure out ways to see Dean at least one other time each week. Poor Muriel--tough as she was, she'd met her match in this kid, especially when Brandi used her many talents to get her way. "I make dinner once or twice a week now, and I make enough to have extra for Dean. Mure hates waste. I try to cook the night before I know Mure needs to go into Portland or on Thursday cuz Friday's a good day to go to the Mall or to the movies or out for pizza. So we can just drop off the plate to Dean, ya know." She laughed happily, and I had to admire her inventiveness.

"So, what do you think is going on with Dean now?" I asked her.

"Well, he's waiting for the sentencing by the judge. He's afraid that he'll have to stay at the Center till he's twenty-one. But I know that won't happen. I know the judge won't make him stay there practically four years--man, that's crazy. Nothin' happened anyway."

"Well, not exactly nothing," I contradicted. "He shot you, even if it was accidental, and injured you. He terrorized several hundred people, not to mention carried a concealed weapon, which is illegal in Maine, and had no permit to use it. Those are some pretty serious offenses."

Brandi shot me a look that definitely would wither a rose. "Yeah, well you know what I mean, Ms. M. Everything's ended up okay. No problem."

I decided to keep my mouth shut rather than mention such not-so-insignificant things as medical costs, court costs, therapy costs, time and money, fear and mistrust. She was in a different place, so I tried a different tact. "How is Dean feeling?"

"I ain't his shrink, Ms. M. Com'on, what do you really want to know?"

"What do you two talk about, I guess," I answered, feeling a little foolish for beating around the rosebush and knowing I should be straightforward.

"Oh, you wanna know what's up with us, huh. Just ask, and I'll tell you. I love Dean, and Dean loves me." I couldn't hide my dismay, and she responded quickly. "Listen, don't go and get your glands in an uproar and definitely don't say nothin' to Mure, cuz she'd go ballistic if she knew. You promised me you're my friend and I can trust you if I tell you things. So you better not rat out." She glared, her blue eyes moist, sparkling like my sapphire earrings.

"All right. I won't go back on my word. But why do you think you love Dean?" I realized as soon as the words were out of my mouth how stupid they sounded--just like a middle-aged dork, as Brandi was fond of calling anyone over thirty.

She ignored the foolishness of my question and answered me in a soft voice. "I love him because he is so gentle and sweet to me. When we spend time together, Dean tells me about his dreams. He wants to be somebody. He's sick of his life, always dodging his father, fighting with everybody, school, smart-ass preps and geeks, and never having anything that's really his. Like he wants to go someplace where nobody knows him, where his father can't find him, and he can be who he wants to be. He loves me and wants me with him when he gets out. And I will be."

"What about Muriel and your life with her? She loves you. And I thought you loved her, too."

"Oh, I do." She paused, shook her head. "I don't know. I wish that Mure liked Dean better. I know she would if she tried to really know him. Then we could all be together, and maybe he wouldn't feel like such a zero. She needs to see how good he really is. There must be some way to get her to see that."

"Is that what you've been trying to do when you get her to go with you to visit Dean? That is what you've been doing, isn't it?" I asked.

"Yeah, well, maybe. But so far she hasn't wanted to spend any time with him. Listen, Ms. M. Both her and you work on losers. Look at me. You both helped me. Help me get her to change her mind about Dean. Please?"

I wondered who was going to help me change my own mind about him, I thought wryly. Obviously, she forgot, or didn't think it mattered, that I didn't like Dean, either. But I certainly didn't want her to think she had no one to turn to for help. If she felt trapped or without resources, she might do something stupid. I knew she realized how lucky she was to have Muriel's support, but I also knew that love, even if she only thought she loved him, could lead her to follow Dean blindly. And he'd proven he had lousy judgment when he was angry or hurt. Maybe I could help them both by keeping an open mind. Maybe I could get Muriel to do the same. After all, she was a professional when it came to working with "bad" kids and trying to bring out the good in them. "All right, kiddo. We'll work on it together."

"Hey, thanks, Ms. M." Brandi jumped up from the bed, knocking her biology book onto the floor, and embraced me in a hug. Wondering what I was getting myself into, I thought about my husband's concern for Dean and decided that he could help me figure out how to persuade Muriel.

If I expected my husband to come up with a complicated plan for how we could get Muriel to like Dean, I was wrong. When I told him about Brandi's request, he said we should just let things take their course. With all the conniving she was up to, it was bound to happen sooner or later. And time was on the kids' side. I decided his advice sounded sensible, and I'd wait and see for now.

3

Dean was sentenced to two years at the Maine Youth Center, with a review to take place after twelve months. Since he'd been at the Center for over four months, that meant he could be released in as short a time as eight months. Brandi, chattering away as we walked through the lobby on our way from the courthouse, was so excited that she walked right into a man standing by the door. Glancing up to excuse herself, she gasped and jumped back. Both Muriel and I turned to see what was wrong.

"You stay away from Dean, you hear," said Mr. Muzzio in a low voice. "I'm warning you."

He was dressed differently from the last time I'd seen him, over three years before. Instead of work clothes, he wore a dark gray suit and a black overcoat. His hair was shorter than I remembered, and he looked more substantial; not just physically since he always was a big man, but he appeared more imposing, more affluent or legitimate, someone to take seriously, at least. I couldn't put my finger on it, but Guy Muzzio seemed to have changed from a big bully to a commanding authority. The old Guy made me uncomfortable, but this one downright frightened me.

I could feel the tension among us, even before Muriel stepped in front of Brandi and spoke to Guy. Her voice was steady, but her hand shook when she reached to take Brandi's arm. "Hello, Mr. Muzzio. I didn't expect to see you here. You weren't in the courtroom. Have you seen Dean?"

"I don't need to see him. I know what the boy looks like." He continued to speak softly, but there was no warmth in his voice. "I came to say something to the little girl here."

"Well, whatever you have to say to her can be said in front of us all."

"I already said what I meant to. Stay away from Dean. You don't belong around him, girl. You're lookin' for trouble if you don't keep your distance. Just remember that."

"That sounds like a threat, Mr. Muzzio," Muriel responded.

"Ain't no threat." He started to turn away, then swung his head back and retorted, "Just good advice." He walked out the door and away before any of us moved.

"He's the one who's no good for Dean, not me. He should keep away from him." Brandi said, but her voice shook.

"You and Brandi get your car and drive around to meet me here at the door. I'm going back in to report this. There's something about that man that really bothers me. I want the authorities informed."

We did as Muriel said, both of us quiet on the walk to the car and on the short drive back to pick her up. I drove to Muriel's car, and we said no more about the incident. On my way home, I recalled the other time I had encountered Mr. Muzzio, when Dean was in my seventh grade class and had threatened the girls at his table and me.

We had met in the principal's conference room to resolve the issue of Dean's classroom behavior. The principal, the guidance counselor, the school social worker, Dean, his parents, and I sat around a large table. The campus police officer was expected but had not arrived. This was my first encounter with Dean's parents; they had not come to the school open house, nor had they attended parent conferences.

Mrs. Muzzio was a pretty woman, fairly tall, with long, dark brown hair, hazel eyes, and a light complexion. I guessed her age to be around thirty. Dean was thirteen, so she must have had him when she was about seventeen, I calculated. Mr. Muzzio was older, mid to late thirties, I figured. Looking at him, I thought I could see Dean in twenty-some years. Mr. Muzzio was extremely good looking: over six feet tall, with an olive complexion, dark, wavy hair threaded with gray strands, brown eyes, a chiseled jaw, and high cheekbones. The red stitching on the pocket of his dark blue work shirt spelled, "Guy." Even dressed in the work shirt and work pants, Guy Muzzio was a compelling presence in that room. I felt a little intimidated, and I sensed that I was not the only uncomfortable staff person. The room was warm, noisy from a lot of chair shuffling, paper rustling, and throat clearing.

The meeting was unpleasant from start to finish. Mr. Muzzio began on the offensive. He pointed at me and said that I had it in for his son. "Dean ain't done nothin' wrong. She's out to get him. What's really wrong is the teacher can't handle kids. Sure, the boy gets outta line sometimes. It just takes a firm hand."

The principal, Mr. Landry, let Mr. Muzzio talk himself out. Then he asked Dean if he had threatened anyone in the class, either the girls or me.

Dean was sitting between his parents; so far he had looked at me only once, his eyes flat and hard. He had spoken a hello in response to greetings by the guidance counselor and the social worker and said nothing more. Looking small seated beside his father, he also appeared pretty much at ease, as if he acquired some strength from Mr. Muzzio, I thought. Before he could answer Mr. Landry, Guy Muzzio cut him off, saying, "He told us he never threatened the teacher. Ain't that right, Ellie?" He looked at his wife.

Mrs. Muzzio answered softly, "Yes."

"Ain't that right, boy? You didn't threaten the teacher, did you?" Mr. Muzzio turned his attention to his son.

"Yeah. I never threatened her." Dean spoke with a sneer in his voice and stared at me with a menacing look. Pressing my sticky hands together in my lap to keep them from trembling, I felt very uncomfortable,

Apparently so did Mr. Landry. "Well," he said. "Seems like we have an impasse here. She says he said, he says she said..."

Just then, Bill Towson, the campus policeman opened the door and entered. "Sorry I'm late, folks," he said and sat in the one unoccupied chair, next to me.

Mr. Landry made the introductions, then addressed Bill. "Mr. Towson, you met with Dean right after the incident in the classroom. What did he say to you?"

"Said he'd been put out of class. When I asked him why, he said the teacher accused him of threatening some students and her. I asked him if he had threatened the teacher. He said yes, he threatened her." Bill repeated what Dean had told him, speaking clearly and smoothly. Apparently he, at least, felt no tension in the situation.

I could have kissed Bill Towson right then and there, despite his beer belly, his gun, his bald head, and his homely face. Suddenly the atmosphere changed. I thought I could detect sighs of relief from the other staff members. I knew Mr. Landry had doubts about the threat and wondered if I hadn't somehow been responsible. After the incident, he'd asked me if I had done anything to provoke Dean, so I knew he would not support me in a standoff with the parents unless someone else backed me up.

Bill went on to repeat almost word for word what I told the group Dean said to me. Since Bill had not been present when I spoke, he had no idea what I'd said. Obviously, he got his information from Dean, who had been honest with Bill about what he had said and done. It was to his father and mother whom he'd lied, or perhaps Guy Muzzio told him what to say in the meeting.

I was relieved and feeling pretty good about my vindication until I looked at Dean and his father. Dean looked like a whipped puppy waiting for the next blow. He seemed to have shrunk further in size. All the starch had left him, and he sat slumped in the chair, his head lowered. The color in Mr. Muzzio's face had deepened a couple of shades, and when I caught his eye, he looked daggers at me. He clenched his teeth and remained quiet during the remainder of the meeting, while Mr. Landry outlined the disciplinary action that would result.

With a sickening feeling, I realized that the real action was going to take place when they got home. Being right and being vindicated suddenly were meaningless to me. I would have received nothing worse than a short lecture on "being more careful when you reprimand students" or something of the sort. Dean was going to get a beating from his father, I was sure.

When the meeting was concluded, Mr. Muzzio stormed out of the office, commanding Dean to "come along" with him. Mrs. Muzzio bade goodbye to everyone and said she was sorry. She looked very unhappy, not meeting anyone's gaze; her voice was constricted, and her hand shook. I didn't see Dean for a week, and, when he did return to class, there were remains of bruises around his eyes and on one cheek.

I reported my suspicions to the guidance office. Even though the social worker tried to get some action taken against Mr. Muzzio, nothing seemed to happen, mostly I guess because both Dean and his mother denied any beatings. They made up some story about falling or hitting something.

If anything resulted from that odd meeting at the courthouse with Mr. Muzzio, it probably was just the opposite from what the man had intended. I don't know whether Muriel's decision was based on his threat, but soon after the hearing, she started letting Brandi see Dean more often, and she began visiting. The next thing I knew she was working exclusively with him, varying her hours so that she was available for Brandi but also able to spend many hours a week at the Center.

Eventually I was asked to tutor Dean. Even though I wasn't sure, I suspected that Muriel was responsible for the request. Maybe Brandi had planted the seed herself, seeing this as a way for us to get to know and to like Dean better.

While reform at the Center was progressing, the area of academics, especially remedial and special needs, still fell short of projected goals set by the Governor's Task Force. Since my school provided tutorial help for all its at-risk students, Dean was eligible to receive the services of a home tutor, or in his case a "Detention Center" tutor, who could take up the slack left by the inadequacies of the Youth Center's current program. Dean stood to benefit from any extra assistance he could receive. When I had expressed my hesitation, telling Muriel that Dean didn't trust me and someone else might be able to reach him more effectively, she encouraged me to take on the task. It was in good part because of her that I became involved with Dean once again.

4

My first visit with Dean did not go well. He was sullen and angry.

"What're you doing here?" he asked me, as I greeted him in the common room of his cottage. He offered no hand to be shaken, as he had done at the courthouse.

"Hi, Dean. I came to see if we could set up a tutoring schedule."

"No way."

"You're entitled to a special tutor to help you keep up with school."

"Yeah, well, not you. Get real, lady." He muttered the last part softly, but I still caught the words.

"I know we've had our differences," I started, thinking I could smooth over the situation. When I looked at him, I stopped. He was staring at me, his eyes hard and flat.

"Just get out. Get the hell out and leave me alone." He stood quickly, his chair falling over backwards and hitting the floor with a crack. Oh, no, I thought to myself, it's like deja vu.

Muriel came into the room then. She must have been expecting some sort of problem and been standing outside the door. "Hey, everything all right here?" she asked.

"It will be when she leaves."

I looked at Muriel, and she nodded her head. I stepped through the door and started walking slowly toward my car, thinking I probably deserved Dean's wrath, although it didn't make me feel any better. As far as he knew, what had I ever done to help him?

Before I got to the parking lot, Muriel caught up with me. "I'm sorry about that," she said.

"Hey, it's not your fault. I guess I forgot that he probably sees me as the enemy."

"Well, give it a few days. I'm sure things will change." She gave me a wink. "I'll be in touch."

True to her word, Muriel called a few days later. "Everything's all set. How would you like to tutor two kids together? We'll make sure you're properly compensated."

"I don't care about the compensation part. Who's the other kid, though?" I asked.

"Someone you know real well. Guess."

"Oh. I get it--Brandi. But, how can that work? She's first year, and he's repeating second year. She's really gifted, and he's remedial."

"You just answered your own question. Individualize. Get Brandi into second year quickly. As you said, she's gifted. With a little motivation, like Dean for instance, she's sure to excel fast. And he'll work his hardest to keep up with her." She laughed. "I guarantee that you won't have any problems with him if she's there."

"Well..."

"It's all set. They're ready for you tomorrow. We'll figure out all the details as we go along. The school's okayed it, and the Center will bend over backwards to cooperate."

My second meeting with Dean succeeded. He did not greet me with open arms or anything, but he was polite. When Brandi punched his elbow, he grunted, "Sorry about the other day."

"That's okay. You had a good reason to resent me. Let's just forget about it." Then we got to work.

I learned very quickly that Dean was remedial in his skills but not in his ability. He'd never attended to lessons and hadn't received help or encouragement at home. His math sense was excellent, and he quickly developed the skills he'd lacked.

The biggest hurdle proved to be getting beyond his fourth grade reading level. Our first task was to improve his comprehension. Brandi's presence made the task tremendously easier for me. She encouraged, bullied, prodded, cajoled, sweet-talked, shouted, and swore at him, and Dean responded amazingly. I wondered if anyone had ever tried this tactic in teaching reading to an adolescent boy.

By spring Brandi had Dean reading the Honors Program list of books with her. At first, she read, while he listened. Eventually, he gained enough confidence to try himself, and she became his best and his worst friend. "Don't be an asshole. You know that word. Just spit it out." "Yeah, that's right. Hey, you may turn into a geek yet. Then what will you say to those grease monkey, dope-head buddies of yours?" "This book is good, I'm tellin' you. Ya gotta get past the beginning and into the good stuff. There's plenty of it too--wait'll you get to the part where they fuc--oops, sorry, Ms. M.--to the love scene. I think you'll like that part. Maybe we better do silent reading there."

Writing was another stumbling block. Again Brandi came to the rescue.

"Just write what you're thinkin', man. I do it all the time. It don't matter if nobody can read it except you. Hey, maybe that's good nobody can read the stuff you write. Ain't nobody gonna read it without your permission--'cept maybe me. So watch out."

I congratulated Muriel and me for Dean's successful academic program. We both believed he and Brandi were benefiting educationally from working together. And they were. Somehow, though, professional as we both were, we failed to consider seriously other ramifications of all the time the two of them spent together--mainly the social, romantic, physical, sexual possibilities. I think I was blinded by my own need to redeem myself with Dean--and to show off how capable Brandi was. I'm not sure about Muriel. I know she loved Brandi dearly. Maybe it was the love that blinded her.

5

By the end of the school year, both Brandi and Dean had demonstrated excellent academic progress; if they continued classes through the summer, she could complete half her sophomore year credits and Dean half of the junior requirements. We'd made a change in his courses so that he was taking college prep classes. Brandi convinced him the extra time involved in changing his program was worth it. "Hey, where're you goin anyway? You're stuck here till the end of the summer at least. And when your hearing comes up, they'll be more likely to let ya out if they think you're a preppie now. College material--yeah."

During the winter, Dean had taken the Driver's Education course and passed the tests. In June he got his driver's license. To celebrate, Muriel, Brandi, Dean, and I went to Lighthouse State Park for a picnic. Dean drove Muriel's car. He was a competent and careful driver, having been behind the wheel of many a car as an adolescent, both with and without his father's permission.

The date of Dean's hearing drew nearer. Since the administrative staff assumed he would be released in September, they extended him more freedom.

He was allowed off the grounds for indefinite periods of time, as long as he returned by ten p.m. Muriel often granted him use of her car when she was working at the Center, and sometimes Brandi went with him. Certainly Muriel knew that they were more than friends, but she trusted Brandi and expected that he would follow her lead. If only it had been that simple.

Brandi and Dean spent a lot of time alone with each other. I wanted to caution her about getting too involved, so I broached the subject the first opportunity I had after the picnic outing. When we finished our tutoring session, I asked her to walk me to my car to pick up a couple of things I had there. On the path I said, "You and Dean are getting close, aren't you?"

"Yup, we're tight."

"It's more than just buddies, I guess?"

"Yup, you guess right."

Obviously, she wasn't going to make it easy for me, so I plunged in. "I hope that you are being sensible, and you're not doing anything foolish or that you'll regret or anything like that."

"I wondered when you were gonna get around to that. So you wanna know if we practice safe sex and everything. I told ya, Ms. M., just be honest with me, and I'll tell you what you wanna know. You should read my journal. You haven't asked to see it in a long time. Afraid? Ha. Just kidding. But I'll go get it right now, and you can take it home with you. Anything ya wanna know or you don't understand, just ask. Ha."

Brandi got her journal for me, and, after I arrived home, I read parts of entries from the past months:

> I never thought things could get any better than they were. I got a real home and like a mother--Muriel. Im doing real good in school. I can't play sports or do much extra activities cuz of physical therapy and tutoring, but that's okay. I never thought I'd have anything like this...
>
> Now my life is perfect. I love Dean and he loves me. Yes. He is sogood to me. I'm the

luckiest person in the world. And Mure likes him. Finally...

When Dean gets out of the Center, probly in September-- 2 months, man that's gonna be great. Maybe he'll be able to get his own car and that will be so cool. I cant wait--we'll go wherever we want and do whatever we feel like. Mure lets Dean have her car for us to go to the movies and stuff and thats cool...

I wanted to go to the drive-in last night but D said he wont go there.

There passion pits. Guys take girls there to have sex. So I said that sounds cool. And Dean said no its not. The girls who go there are whores and the guys have no respect for them anyway. So we went to Maine Cinema.

~~~~~~~~~~~

I finally asked D why he didn't think I was sexy. He said whatta ya talkin' about. Your the sexiest girl I know. I said well you don't show it. He said can't you tell by how I look at you and how I hold you and kiss you? And I said well yeah but how come you always stop before we do anything. I dont wanna stop. He said Look Brandi. I love you. I could spend the rest of my life loving you. And Im not gonna fuck that up. I dont want what happened to my mother to happen to you. She got pregnant when she was 16 and her life got ruined. I said well she got you so it wasnt totally ruined. D got pissed and said Im tryin to be serious Brandi. Dont screw around. I said. You wont let me. Your damn right I wont. Not till we get married. And then he stopped. It was quiet for a while. Then I said if thats a proposal I accept.

And he said it is but I didn't think you would want me. And I said your all I want. So I guess I might be a virgin when I get married but thats okay cuz if thats what D wants I guess that's what I want too.

I laughed to think that Muriel and I had been worried about the wrong kid. Brandi was ready for anything--it was Dean who was holding back. Another part of me still worried. Both of them were too young to be thinking anything as serious as marriage. Wanting to warn Muriel, I knew I had to keep my peace because I'd promised not to divulge the contents of the journal.

PART FOUR

1

Dean's hearing with the judge coincided with the start of the school year in September. Commenting that he was impressed with his progress at the Youth Detention Center, the judge indicated the biggest concern was where Dean would live. Since the Muzzios had signed a form allowing the court to designate a custodial guardian upon his release from the Center, the judge said that Dean needed an appropriate place with the right atmosphere to enable him to continue his rehabilitation. "It has been brought to my attention that a place exists in the home of Mr. and Mrs. Ryan, who are willing to take responsibility for providing room, board, and supervision. Are the Ryans present this morning?" Receiving an answer in the affirmative, he continued, "Please come forward then, and we'll discuss this matter."

Tom Ryan, the wrestling coach at the high school, was almost a legend, both as a great coach and as a wonderful mentor for troubled teenage boys. He and his wife, Elizabeth, had sheltered kids and taken on their problems for years. In their mid-fifties, they had no children of their own and dedicated themselves to wrestling and to kids. If Dean could make it anywhere in the community, Coach Ryan's would be the place.

After discussing the matter with the Ryans, the court representative, and Muriel, as the caseworker, the judge addressed Dean. "You've heard our discussion and the expectations placed on you. Are you satisfied with the arrangements, son?"

"Yes, Sir, I am," he answered, speaking in a clear voice and looking the judge in the eye. A far different person from the crazy kid who had stormed the school gym a little over a year ago, he amazed me at his transformation. He stood to his full height of six feet, no slouching as if he'd like to disappear. The eye contact and the direct talk were a big improvement over the sullen mumbling or defiant threatening of the past. He certainly looked handsome and clean-cut in pressed khakis, a new shirt, a tie, and a brown blazer.

I glanced at Brandi, sitting to my right, to see her reaction to the proceedings. Her face reflected her feelings pretty clearly: she was beaming, her blue eyes glistening and her color as blushed as the rose sweater she wore. Turning her head to look at me, she whispered, "This is so great."

Dean's year at the Youth Center had prepared him well for his return to high school. His writing skills needed more work, and he enrolled in a composition class, but his reading ability soared, and he had read the Honors Program novels. So he chose an advanced literature course but took the writing assignments to the composition teacher for individual instruction.

When teachers encountered the "new" Dean Muzzio, they were so pleasantly surprised they generally overextended themselves to make things work for him. The school still wanted me to tutor, so teachers would tell me the instant they noticed even the minutest problem in his work.

For the first few weeks, Dean rode to school with Coach Ryan, who convinced him to join the junior varsity wrestling team. "There probably won't be a place on the varsity team for a while, but work out, get to know the guys, come to the meets, and eventually you'll make varsity," he told Dean. Mr. Ryan found him a job on the weekends. In early October Coach helped him acquire an old Chevy pickup, its blue paint peeling everywhere, but in good running condition, especially after Dean's knowledgeable tinkering on it. Things were going well.

2

I did not see a lot of Brandi that fall but knew she took a cross-section of courses the way that Dean did. In fact, they were in the same advanced literature section, although she didn't need the composition class. Instead she enrolled in creative writing. Having filled so many notebooks with journal entries, she was a natural for the regimen of a writing program.

Brandi became manager of the varsity wrestling team, which didn't come as a surprise to me, considering Dean's involvement with the team. I heard from Elizabeth Ryan that she took over in her commanding style, and most of the boys were cowed by her demands and general bossiness. It sounded to me like both of them were much too busy to revert to their self-destructive behavior.

Sitting at my desk one mid-October morning, I looked up to see Brandi standing before me, a smirk on her face. An old cigarette slogan came into my head: "You've come a long way, Baby!"

"Yo, Ms. M., what's happenin?' Ya got any punks ya need dealin' with? Here I am."

"You don't look much like one to be taking on a punk," I laughed.

At fifteen and a half, she'd become a stunning young lady. Not a beauty-- there were many more attractive high-school girls-- she, nevertheless, possessed a presence. It occurred to me that she'd always had that quality, although in the past she used it with negative results. Now charm, a zest for life, seemed to spill onto anyone in her vicinity. And she'd turned into a real cutie. She stood about 5'5", without the old clunky shoes, and weighed maybe a hundred and ten pounds. Longer now, her hair was thick, shiny, and healthy, a little less blonde than the year before. "I stopped helpin' the sun cuz Dean said he liked my natural highlights better," she told me. It fell just below her shoulders, although she wore it in a ponytail much of the time. Just pale gloss slicked her lips, and mascara showcased those big, blue, saucer eyes.

Brandi's wardrobe had undergone a significant overhaul since the first day when I had seen her on top of Denise in that fight. From what I'd noticed lately, nothing she had was baggy or oversized. Her jeans fit well, and the tees often were form-fitting, outlining a well-proportioned body.

On the day of a game or a meet, it was a practice at the high school for male athletes to wear a tie and jacket and for female athletes to jettison the usual jeans for a skirt or a dress. Since managers were considered part of the team, they followed the tradition. Standing in my room that fall day, Brandi wore a short skirt, stockings, and flats.

"Yeah, well punks don't interest me anymore. I got more important things to do," she said. Then, twirling in front of me, she asked, "Well, how do I look? We have a meet today."

"The skirt's a little short for whirling around in, but other than that, I think you look very nice. What do you think?"

"Dean says I really look tough when I dress up, and he likes fuzzy sweaters and low heels cuz it makes me more huggable, he says. So, okay, I can handle that. No problem."

"I guess that means you like the way you look."

She chortled, underscoring her answer. "Yeah, I do, Ms. M., I do."

"So, what are you up to these days--other than Dean, classes, Dean, wrestling, and Dean?"

"You're a real comedian, Ms. M. Well, those things sure keep me busy. But, hey, guess what? I'm working on the school newspaper, and I'm writing for the literary journal. A little thing I wrote is gonna be in the next one."

"That's wonderful. What's it about? I'd love to read it."

"Well, it just so happens I have it right here. Actually, I was hopin', if you're not too busy, that is, maybe you could take a look and make sure it's okay. It's been accepted, but I just thought you might make sure I haven't made any stupid mistakes or anything that nobody noticed."

"I'd be happy to read it and check it for you, too, Kiddo," I said.

"Okay, then. Cool. I'll leave it here, and you can call me or somethin' after you look at it. Hey, I gotta get back to the high school.. I have a class in five minutes. If I don't run, I'll be late."

"You better not run too fast in that skirt, or some guy might get the wrong idea."

"No way. After I decked him, Dean'd finish him off. Nobody messes with the team of Brandi and Dean. Ha. Hey, see ya around, Ms. M. And thanks." She treated me to one of her dazzling smiles, then was gone as quickly as she'd appeared.

I didn't wait until evening to look at Brandi's essay. Right after school was over, I read the piece:

Memory

My memory is a blueprint that I can draw. It's a long walk from the white house on top of the hill. It's the pond we walk by with its willow tree-covered island in the middle, the pond full of turtles and huge burping, green bullfrogs. It's the blueberry fields at the bottom of the hill, acres of tall, shiny-leaved bushes loaded down with fleshy blue buttons.

Memory is the skin-soaking wetness of grass I walk in with my mother on a summer morning. It's my brown rubber boots squishing along the soggy furrows between the blueberry bushes. Disgusting Japanese beetles crawling on my fingers. It's the galvanized pail, secured around my middle with brown twine, thownking against my belly. It hurts where it cuts into my waist.

It's the sound of the of the first few blueberries dropping into the pail. Ping, plink, pong; pretty soon no more ping, plink, pong, as the bottom disappears. It's picking until my shorts stick to my legs and my bottom, where they brush up against the bushes. Pail not filling fast enough.

How many berries should I pick today, Mama? Too many, I think, wanting to quit before I've hardly started. Sticking out my bluish tongue, waving my purpley hands and fingers, I pretend that I live in the Land of the Purple People-Eaters.

by Brandi Buckman-Robb

I wondered whether Brandi remembered the incident she wrote about. Had she ever picked blueberries with her mother? Or was she creating a happy childhood experience for herself? I also noted her signature at the end of the essay and smiled. The bond between Muriel and her had strengthened over the almost two years that they had known each other. I'm not sure who first had the idea of adoption, since each claimed it was her decision. Brandi had taken to signing her last name Buckman, leaving Robb tagged on the end, at first so teachers would not be confused and later, "to remind me who I used to be and where I'm goin'. I'll drop Robb when the adoption is official."

Muriel had hired an attorney who completed all the preliminaries before Christmas break. The final requirement was to run an announcement of intent in the Portland newspaper. Since Brandi's mother was dead and her father unknown, unnamed in any records the lawyer had researched, the ad was an unimportant but necessary final step. Adoption could take place sixty days later, and Muriel was planning a special celebration in early March for their big day.

3

Meanwhile, winter gripped the area. January could be dismal in northern New England, with limited daylight, the temperature often below zero for days at a time, and constant storm threats. For the most part, snow actually made life easier. Highway crews, adept at snow removal, quickly cleared the roads once a storm abated. Without snow I'm not sure how people could avoid "cabin fever," that claustrophobic feeling resulting when one can't get out and about. Coping with winter was much easier with an abundance of snow. Alpine and cross-country skiing, snowmobiling, and ice fishing allowed many an otherwise housebound person a healthy outlet, while making good use of the wintry conditions.

My husband and I spent the month doing our share of skiing, but we took in an occasional wrestling meet. Dean had stuck with his practices and benefited from another wrestler's misfortune. Dan Mason, who wrestled varsity in the same weight category, dislocated his shoulder during a practice over the holidays, and Dean won a three-way competition for the spot.

One Friday night in late January, we attended a home meet, sat with Muriel, and watched Dean work a tough opponent to the mat for a pin. At the end of the evening, her duties completed, Brandi bounded over to us as we waited in the hall. "Your team did a nice job." I said in greeting her. "Dean really is doing well, I see."

"Yeah, he's my man. Yo, Mure, you didn't spill the beans, did you?"

"I kind of thought you'd probably want to tell Ms. M. yourself," Muriel said, smiling.

"Okay, what are you talking about?" I asked.

"Well, Ms. M., you're lookin' at the first place winner of the Young Authors Short Story Contest. That all," Brandi answered me in a rush of words. "And guess what? The prize is...an All Expenses Paid Trip to...Disneyland. For two. So we're goin' February vacation. What'd ya think of that?"

"I'm impressed. Congratulations. That's really a wonderful tribute to your writing. So you and Muriel are going to California."

"Yep, we are. And Dean's comin' with us."

I looked at Muriel. She said, "It seemed like a nice way to celebrate a lot of things. And Dan Mason will be wrestling by then, so Dean will be sent down to J.V., which will be finished with their meets by vacation."

"Mure and I are taking the room the contest pays for, and she's payin' for a room for Dean," Brandi said. "She's also payin' for his plane ticket."

"That's pretty generous," I commented.

Muriel laughed. "Well, I don't think I was officially invited. This way I get to play chaperone. And Dean is paying for part of his trip."

"Oh, Mure, I know we couldn't have gone alone, anyway. You fixed it so there was a way he could come." Brandi hugged Muriel, then spun around as Dean approached us, looking particularly handsome with his curly black hair glistening from the damp of the shower.

"Hey," he greeted us. "Brandi and I're going for pizza. You all can come with us."

Later that night, I voiced my concern to my husband about Muriel letting Dean go with them to California, worried that it might give them the idea they could indulge their physical relationship. He made light of it, saying that, if they wanted to do something, they didn't need a trip across the country to accomplish it. They had more than enough opportunity right around home. Trucks worked just great for that kind of thing.

The next time I saw Brandi was the Thursday after February break. She stopped by my room to drop off a copy of the *Young Authors' Anthology*, which contained her short story. "How was Disneyland?" I asked.

"Awesome. This was the first time I've been out of the state and the first time I flew in a plane, too. I have to finish an article for the newspaper and study for an exam, so I gotta run. In case you're interested in readin' about my trip, I brought my journal."

"You know I'm interested. Thanks very much. I'll finish reading it this weekend and get it back to you by next Monday. Okay?"

"No problem, Ms. M. See you Monday."

A blizzard swept in Friday night and continued until early Sunday. On Saturday morning I settled in to read Brandi's journal of her trip to Disneyland:

I got a new journal just for the trip. It's really pretty with a map of the world like all over and then little pictures of places. This trip was a whole collection of firsts--my first time out of Maine, first airplane ride (maybe the best part, but it's hard to pick only one best part), first meal up in the sky, first time in a hotel, first rooftop swimming pool, first time at Disneyland of course, first time going on a vacation, and first time going away with my boyfriend. It's the first time for all these things for Dean too--it's like we're a couple of backwoods dweebs. But I don't care, it's so totally awesome.

Mure was sooo cool. I thought we'd all sit together on the plane, but this plane had 2 seats together, 4 seats, and then 2 seats across. Mure got a 2 seat section for Dean and me, and she sat in a seat in front of us—not even behind us to spy on us or anything. I mean it was so awesome cuz we pretended we were this couple flying across the country by ourselves. Dean was as excited as I was, but he acted cooler. I really loved it when we ate dinner right at our seats. These trays come down out of the back of the seat in front, and then the stewardess gives you a tray with a whole dinner on it. I had chicken, Dean had pasta.

Disneyland was totally awesome. We went to so many cool things—the Indiana Jones ride, Jungle Cruise, Fantasy Fireworks, Country Bear Show--just amazing. I don't know what I liked best. It's a Small World was dorky, but I really like it. Even the teacups, which is a little kids thing, was so cute. We stayed at the Disneyland Hotel and rode the monorail back and forth to the park. The hotel has a swimming pool on the roof—so cool. It was so much warmer than Maine--I mean like summer in comparison. There weren't a lotta people swimming in the pool, but Dean and I did everyday. It's heated and all, too, so it was really great.

Dean and I had a lot of time to talk--to really get into some deep stuff. Like his family. He hasn't seen his mother for a while. She sneaks to meet him sometimes and calls him, but she has to do it behind Mr. Muzzio's back cuz he'd go ballistic if he found out. He is such a @#$% I feel sorry for his mother and for Dean. Dean really loves her, but she is so afraid of his father because he hurts her when he gets mad. When Dean lived with them, sometimes he would get between them and let his father beat on him to protect his mother.

I can't imagine letting some guy do that to me. Dean is so different from his father. He's changed so much. He has never hit me or even threatened to or anything like that. He's so gentle now, really. I'm glad I got shot--well, I don't mean that really. I'm not glad I got shot. I mean I'm glad that we found each other even if it had to happen the way it did.

We had a long talk one night in the lobby of the hotel. We were sitting in this plushy lounge pretending we were these rich people on a vacation. We sat there half the night and just talked and talked. I understand a lot better now why Dean won't do anything besides a lot of kissing and a little bit more. He told me that his mother probably never would have married his father if he hadn't got her pregnant. It was almost like he raped her—she was like 15, same as me, and she went out with him some but she didn't want to hook up with him or anything. But he was so pushy and wouldn't take no for an answer. And then she got pregnant and was so scared and everything, and they got married. Her father like almost made them do it. He was totally ballistic when he found out and he told Mr. Muzzio to marry his daughter or he would kill him. Then Mr. Muzzio took it out on her. It's such an awful story. I guess Dean's mother told him one time after a big fight with his father.

Well, anyway, the trip was amazing--for the great time at Disneyland and the plane and all--but also because Dean and I got closer.

My fears about Dean and Brandi getting too involved physically were allayed. I shared the essence of the journal with my husband, who basically said, "I told you so."

4

During the last week of February, shocking news hit Brandi head-on. I was still at school on Thursday afternoon when the phone rang, and answering it, I recognized Muriel's voice, sounding distraught. "I need your help. The lawyer handling the adoption called, and I need to find Brandi. Can you see if she's anywhere around? I called the high school and had her paged, but she didn't respond. Maybe she didn't hear the page."

"Sure, I'll look around. You sound terrible. What's wrong?"

"A man who said he saw the announcement about the adoption in the paper called Brian McKee. Said he didn't care if I adopt Brandi, but he wants to talk to her and Dean. When Brian asked him what it was about, the man said it was private. Then he asked who was calling, and the man hung up. I don't know what it's all about, but I'm worried."

My search did not turn up Brandi or Dean. One of their friends told me they left school and probably had headed home. I called my husband, and he met me at Muriel's house after work, and the three of us waited together for Brandi to return.

Around seven, she called, hysterical. Muriel got her to say where she was, and we drove to get her, at a convenience store on the outskirts of Portland.

At first, Brandi was incoherent. Clothes rumpled, hair a mess, face red and splotchy, she sobbed for a long while after she got into the car. It wasn't until we were back at the house and Muriel had helped her into pajamas, washed her face and hands, and made a cup of hot chocolate that Brandi settled down enough to tell us what was going on.

"Nothing could be worse even if a bomb exploded or a car ran me over. I can't live without Dean. And I'm scared."

"Brandi, start at the beginning and tell us what happened," Muriel said.

She sniffled a little, then began to talk: "Dean had some stuff to take to the wrestling barn for Coach, so we did that. We hung out with Mrs. Ryan for a while, then I remembered I needed a new cartridge for my printer, so we were goin' to Staples to get it. After we got gas at the Big Apple, Dean drove behind by the dumpster so he could toss out some junk from the back of the truck.

We were just getting ready to leave when his father pulled up next to us. I don't know how he saw us back there, but he musta recognized the truck or something. I said to Dean let's get outta here and we started to get in the truck, but Mr. Muzzio came over and blocked my door so I couldn't get in

'I saw in the paper that cop's adopting you,' he said.

'She's not a cop, yeah, and what business is it of yours?' I asked.

'I got this piece a paper here says somethin' about lookin' for next of kin.' He pulled a dirty piece of newspaper outta his back pocket.

'So what,' I said and tried to push past him, but he wouldn't let me.

Dean had came over to my side of the truck by then and told his father to get outta the way.

'Got somethin' you oughtta know,' he said.

'There's nothin' you could tell us that would interest us,' Dean said.

'Wanna bet? You been screwin' her?' he nodded at me.

'Shut up, you asshole. You're drunk,' Dean yelled at him.

'You better watch out, boy. Unless, that is, you wanna keep it in the family.'

'What the fuck you talkin' about, dickhead?' Dean hollered.

Dean's father turned back to me and said, 'You look just like your mother. She was a pretty little thing, a real tease. I couldn't keep my hands off her. But she was dumb, like you.'

I started to get this sick feeling in my stomach. 'What are you talking about, I asked. You didn't know my mother.'

'I knew your mother real good. Yeah. Guess what, boy? This here's your little sister. How do ya like that?' He started to laugh, this awful, ugly sound, and then Dean hit him. They started fighting, but Dean's a lot stronger now since he's been wrestling. And Mr. Muzzio was so drunk he was having a hard time even standing up straight. After he quit fighting back, Dean kept hitting and hitting him, pounding on his head and chest. He was crying and yelling, and I was afraid he was going to kill his father. Finally, I got him to stop. Mr. Muzzio was just lying kinda half in and half out of the bushes behind the dumpster. I thought maybe Dean already killed him.

We got in the truck, and he peeled out and was driving crazy, like, he never does that. We both were crying. Finally I said, 'What are we gonna do,' and Dean said he had to get away and think. I told him I was going with him, and he said no. Right by the entrance to 95, he pulled over into the Cumberland Farms and told me to get out. I said no way. He came around to my side, pulled me out, got in and locked that door, and got behind the wheel and peeled out again. I was running after him, yelling and crying and everything, but he wouldn't stop. He got on the highway. I ran to the ramp and started up, but then I knew he wasn't gonna come back for me, so I went back to the Cumberland Farms, and then I called you.

Oh, my God, Mure, what am I gonna do? I'm so scared--he was acting crazy when he left. How can his father be my father? We love each other."

Muriel could not get Brandi to go to bed, so she bundled her up and let her lie on the couch while she called Tom Ryan. Luckily, he was at home, and Muriel filled him in on the situation while Elizabeth listened on the extension. Coach Ryan said he would get someone he trusted to check the whereabouts and the condition of Guy Muzzio. Muriel said she would call around to see if Dean might have gone to a friend's house, but Brandi said, "He's not at anybody's house. He said he wanted to be alone."

Elizabeth said she thought she knew where he might have headed. "We have a camp out past Greenville. Dean's been to it with Tom. If he wanted to be by himself, I think he'd go there. There's no phone or electricity, and the road would be open only part way in at this time of year."

Tom said, "I think Elizabeth's right. I don't want to call anyone down there and risk making him edgier. We'll go ourselves. I'll have my friend get back to you when he finds out about Guy. You better call your lawyer, Muriel, and tell him what's happened. I'm not sure, but you may need to inform the police about this, too. Do whatever the lawyer says. We'll call you from Greenville after we've checked at camp. It'll take us about four hours."

After getting Muriel to promise she would call us if she needed anything, we went home, but I slept little that night, worrying about both Brandi and Dean. On Friday morning, the weather was as downcast as my spirits. The sky was heavy with storm clouds, which occasionally sent down sleet or dripping flakes of snow. The day slogged along this way, and late Saturday evening Muriel called to say that the Ryans had found Dean at camp. Guy Muzzio turned up in the county jail in Alton, picked up by the sheriff's department in the wee hours of Friday morning, after he ran his car off the road and hit a tree. He demolished the car, banged himself up, and had been charged with operating a vehicle while under the influence of alcohol. Nothing had been mentioned about any fight.

As ludicrous as the story Guy Muzzio told seemed, maybe it was true: it was possible that he had dated Brandi's mother, took advantage of her, and actually could be her father. The story reminded me of something that happened to me as a child. It bothered me as an adult to a far greater extent than ever it had when I was young. Then, what had happened seemed, if not completely normal, at least not shameful or wrong. Now the memory rankled so much that I basically had expunged it from my conscious. It came back to taunt me now, though. While what happened to me bore little significance or had the tangible consequences that Mr. Muzzio's actions had on Brandi's mother, it just proved to me that nice girls were at risk even with boys they knew and probably trusted; unfair things could and did happen. So Mr. Muzzio's story just could be the truth, I thought.

5

Muriel and the Ryans let the school know that Dean and Brandi were involved in a sensitive situation and would be absent from school for an indefinite period of time. Without knowing all the details, the administration handled the issue innovatively and discretely. Both students had progressed tremendously, academically and socially, so everyone was eager to help.

The unique manner in which the school approached the matter resulted from the reform process the school board initiated as a result of the probation handed down to the high school by the Accreditation Committee. The administration had five years to rectify all deficient areas and to meet certain specific standards. One of the requirements was to develop a system that outlined criteria for comprehensive educational excellence. The school board had to show the changes it would make and why, how it would make them, and then document all attempts, successful or not.

A large corporation headquartered in Portland recently had joined with the school district in a partnership, part of a national thrust by business and industry to become active in the preparation of the next generation of workers. The benefit to schools involved in a business partnership included liaison personnel, teacher assistance, student mentors, and money. The business demanded accountability, which generally guaranteed good planning, development, and follow-through.

The school board and the corporation decided to initiate a program originally developed by business interests to meet their needs and customized by academicians to apply to educational settings which identified all aspects of a school setting in business-related terms, such as producer (administration, faculty, staff), client (students, parents), and product (curriculum, program of study). Schools would provide anything a student needed in order to succeed, whether that meant a college-credit course, an electric wheelchair, a one-on-one aide, French lessons, modernized labs, or asbestos-free classrooms.

Literally, for Brandi and Dean, the program meant that the school remained cognizant of their individual circumstances and provided accordingly. The first consideration was how best to provide for their educational needs.

Thus, when Dean ran off and Brandi stayed at home, the administration worked out a plan to ensure that their education would not be interrupted. They also listened to Muriel, to the

Ryans, to Brian McKee, and to the social workers and the psychologists who had been working with the kids. They listened to Brandi and would have listened to Dean, had he been available. The plan they set up was based on input from everyone and could be amended as needed.

Although he refused to leave camp, Dean was willing to have the Ryans stay with him. Tom took on the task of tutoring him so he could keep up with his studies, and the school hired a substitute to handle Tom's classes at the high school. Since Brandi believed she couldn't face school right away without Dean, I served as her tutor and as liaison between her and her teachers.

Brian McKee, the lawyer handling Brandi's adoption, advised Muriel to go ahead with the adoption as soon as possible, in case Dean's father decided to contest it. He also advised Muriel to hire a private detective to investigate the circumstances surrounding the pregnancy of Barbara Richardson, Brandi's birth mother. He told her, "A DNA test is the only conclusive way to determine if Muzzio's telling the truth, but you would need his permission. I suggest exploring every other possible means of discovering the biological father before trying to convince him to submit to testing."

Brandi wanted to proceed with the adoption, but she decided against having the grand celebration Muriel originally had planned. Nothing more was heard from Guy Muzzio about his alleged paternity or about any objection to the adoption, and the ceremony took place quietly in early March in the judge's chamber. Brian McKee and I served as witnesses, and my husband was a spectator. Brian took everyone to dinner afterwards.

Both Muriel and Brandi were happy, but Brandi was subdued. "You know how grateful I am that you saved my life, Mure," she said. "I'd probably be back in the Center or maybe dead if you didn't take me in. I only love two people--you're one of them." She broke down then, and Muriel embraced her.

Sobbing, she hugged Muriel, who said, "We'll work this out somehow."

"I'm so glad I got you."

"That's good, kid, because there's no way you'll ever get rid of me."

As her tutor again, I got to see Brandi regularly through the rest of the school year. She would not even consider going back to school. "How can I when every place I go there reminds me of Dean? I'll do my schoolwork and whatever else you want, but don't make me go back to school. I just can't do it."

She was a different girl that spring. The smiles were rare, and I don't think I heard her laugh once all the times I was with her. I think her course work provided a way for her to forget her troubles, to lift the blanket of despair that covered her most of the time, and she excelled in her studies. Accomplishing a lot of writing during this time, she offered me her journal to read whenever I wanted. Many of the entries were about Dean. She wrote often about the effect of learning that Guy Muzzio was her father. When I read some of her entries, I saw that Brandi had not let the shocking discovery consume her:

> I just wanted to die. How could anything so horrible happen to anybody? Either there is no God or else he is the nastiest sicko. How could he let Dean and me fall in love with each other and then let us have the same father? And such a disgusting father--I want to puke just thinking about it. But then I remember that Dean's had him for a father all his life, and he's turned out real good, especially with all the help from Coach and Elizabeth. I feel bad then that I'm so mad. It's a bigger mess for Dean. I have Mure. He has Coach and Elizabeth to help him, but it's not the same--Muriel is my adopted mother now and nobody can take me away from her.
>
> Dean still is stuck with Guy and Ellie, and they could do something bad to him, like make him come back or make him leave the Ryans. He can't really be safe from his father till he's 18--and that's more than a year away, or Guy could try to hurt him again. Plus, Muriel is like my real and only mother. I love, Love, LOVE her. Dean doesn't have any parent like that. He's got a wishy washy mother and a @#$% creep for a father."

Another entry several pages later:

> Not talking to Dean is killing me. "Killing Me Slowly" Actually its killing me fast. Why Why WHY wont he answer my letters or call me or Something. I think maybe he blames me for being his sister. But I didn't know, and I sure dont want it to be. I dont want to be Dean's sister, dammit-- I want to be his girlfriend and someday his lover and then maybe his wife. Oh, God, his wife. Now that will never happen. But I'll take anything I can have of him. I'll do anything just to be around him. Doesn't he understand that? Please dont reject me Dean because of your father. Dont you see how he wins if you do that? I need you--anyway you let me be with you I'll do it. Just dont ignore me. Please

6

When school ended in the middle of June, we decided to take a break from tutoring and schoolwork. Brandi had earned A's in every course, including a senior level literature seminar and a creative writing class for which she received three college credits through the University.

"Enough of the academics for a while," Muriel said, when the three of us celebrated Brandi's report card over dinner at Old Country Buffet. Nobody wanted to go there. As Brandi had said, "That place is okay when you're a kid and don't know any better, but really it sucks big time."

"With that language, it sounds like the place you belong. Besides, I think we should go there just to reminisce about the old days."

"Oh. You wish they were back?" she asked.

"Good God, no. That girl was a diamond in the rough, true enough. But I certainly don't want to return to the mines. Do you?"

"No, definitely not."

"But it seems appropriate to celebrate how far you've come."

So we sat in the cavernous, glorified cafeteria while Muriel shared a plan she had thought up. "This kid needs to have some fun." Brandi made a face but didn't say anything. "And I need a vacation. I made reservations for us to go on a windjammer cruise."

"What is that?"

"For an intelligent girl, you are pretty unknowledgeable. You've lived in Maine all your life, and you don't know what a windjammer is? Well, see if you can find out before we go next week."

"Aw, com'on, Mure, you said no cracking books for the summer. Just tell me."

"Okay, I guess I can do that this time. A windjammer is a sailing ship. Maine has several of them that take passengers from Rockland out around the islands along the coast for about a week. They don't have a set plan—they go by the weather, stopping at different ports for the night and just cruising the waters. You can help with the sailing or other crew chores if you want or you can just relax, swim, read, play cards, sleep, whatever fancies you."

"Yeah, that sounds neat. I'd like that. Thanks, Mure."

"Oh, and I thought we'd go to Coach Ryan's camp at Moosehead on the way back--see what it looks like. He's bragged about it to me for so many years, it's time I checked it out."

Brandi dropped her forkful of pasta and stared, her eyes opening from their usual saucers to practically dinner plate size. "Are you serious? Do you think it's all right? I mean, what about Dean? He hasn't answered any of my letters, definitely hasn't called--as far as I know, he couldn't care less if I dropped dead." She tried to keep her voice light, but tears had formed in her eyes and threatened to spill out. She wiped them with her napkin.

Muriel put her hand on Brandi's arm. "I wouldn't suggest it if he didn't agree. And Tom and Elizabeth think he's ready to deal with his father's demons."

"Oh, so he thinks I'm a demon. Great."

"I didn't put that right. You aren't the demon. The demons are in Dean's head, same as they are with you. The only difference is you've wanted to talk about it and work things out right from the beginning. He needed time to sort through his feelings and figure out how he felt—not about you, but about himself, about his father, about the shock of learning you might be his half-sister..."

"Whadda ya mean, might be?" Brandi cut in. "Guy said he and my mother...shit...he's my father."

"Well, yes, he said that, and it may be so. But there's reason to think he might have been lying."

"Lying? That's a pretty sick thing to lie about," Brandi raised her voice.

"Think about it. Guy Muzzio is a loser. He's got nothing except his perverted pleasure in controlling his son. When Dean moved in with the Ryans and started to turn his life around, Guy was angry. He wanted to get back at Dean. He can't beat him up anymore--Dean's stronger than he is. So he might--mind you, might. I'm not completely sure yet that it isn't true--he might have made up this story about being your father because it was the one thing he could think of that would devastate his son."

"He sure was right about that," she said. "But what makes you think it all might be a lie? You never said anything to me before."

"I didn't know anything before. But I've been working with Brian McKee and a private investigator. They've found out quite a bit about your mother and the situation surrounding your birth. Things are looking more and more likely--only likely, not definite," Muriel said, as Brandi grinned and started to rise from her chair, "that Guy Muzzio isn't your biological father. We should know in a short while, maybe by the time we go to camp. "

"Oh."

"So I wanted to let you know and prepare you for the possibility, either way it falls out. The Ryans have talked to Dean, and he's ready to handle the outcome, whatever it is. He's ready to face you and talk it out, finally."

"Oh, Mure. What if it's not true? I know, I know. It's still probably true. But at least I can see him and talk. And, if I can talk to him, I know I'll be able to get him to see that it doesn't matter if we are related. We still love each other, and we should be together."

I must have stiffened visibly or shone a reaction on my face because Brandi looked at me and continued, "Chill out, Ms. M. I'm not talking about hooking up or anything incestuous like that. I mean we care a lot about each other, and we can work out the rest. If we're brother and sister, we should love each other. It's different, but it's not that different. We aren't going to screw around— whoops, sorry—have physical relations, something kinky like that, but we still have feelings. And being sister and brother means we should stay close. That's what I mean."

"Oh," I said.

"I have a good feeling about this vacation." She smiled, the first big, happy smile I'd seen from her since winter.

I worked on a few projects around my home after school ended. I did not see Brandi again until late in August, just before school resumed. She called me one evening and asked if she could drop by. We had a lot to catch up on, she said.

Brandi arrived alone. "I have my license now, so I can drive myself around. It's great. And Mure says maybe I can get my own wheels when school starts."

"So you're planning to go back to school this fall," I commented.

"Yeah, I'm definitely ready. I needed to be by myself and get my head together before. But I'm okay now. Knowing the truth about my birth parents is such a relief. I sometimes thought I would go nuts with all the questions I had running around in my head." She stopped and looked at me closely. "You don't know how it turned out, do you?"

"No, I don't. You're so serious, I think I can guess, though. You seem to be handling it very maturely."

"Yeah, I've grown up a lot since last winter," she said.   Then she started to laugh. "I psyched you out, lady. Guy Muzzio is not, I repeat, not, not, not my biological father. Hallajulah. I was so relieved when I found out that I could have kissed that chubby little Mr. McKee. I really think I was ready to accept it if he was, but thank God I don't have to."

"That's wonderful, kiddo. So he lied all along."

"Well, he didn't outright lie. He didn't exactly know. I mean it wasn't really likely that he was, but he'd been with my mother and they'd hooked up once. You know, he was married then, the scumbag, so he even cheated on his wife. And Dean was a baby then. So, anyway, there was a remote possibility. But my mother had a boyfriend, and she never told, I guess, and neither did Guy about them hooking up, so nobody knew except her and him, not even my mother's boyfriend. His name, incidentally, was Pete.

"Was?"

"He's dead. Died in a car crash somewhere way Down East even before I was born."

"So both of your real parents aren't living."

"My real mother is Mure. My biological parents aren't living."

"Oh, of course. Sorry."

"No problem, Ms. M. It takes a while to get used to all the ways to say it. I'm really glad nobody at school knows about all the shit that went down last year. I'd really hate having to go through all this crap with them. It's better that they think Dean and his father had a big fight and Dean got hurt and went away and that I was so upset I couldn't come to school."

"Is that what they think?" I asked.

"Yup, pretty much."

"So. How did Mr. McKee find out the truth?"

"Well, it's pretty complicated. I don't understand it all myself. They know Dean's father isn't my father because of something about the blood. They got a blood sample from me, my mother's was on her records at the hospital or somewhere--I don't know where all the information came from, the private dick did that stuff-- and Guy's been in so many brawls and stuff I guess his is available everywhere. Well, I guess his type and my mother's weren't compatible or else the kind they have couldn't make what I have or something--I'm not sure exactly. But I know the blood stuff really was a lucky thing. Because of the weirdness of it all, they didn't have to try to do DNA. They would've had to get Guy's permission for that. And he probably wouldn't have let them."

"That's good it worked out," I said. "But how did they find out who the real--I mean the biological--father was?"

"The private eye did a lot of talking around and record searching and stuff. I don't think there were many people who knew anything much, but he got a little bit of information from a couple of people. He wouldn't say who they were. Then some confidential files he sort of saw or something fishy, cuz he has some friends in the "right places," as he said, who confirmed what he'd been told. Then he matched up what he found there with all the stuff he got on Pete. And that's how he figured it out. Or something like that. Like I said, I only care that that dirt bag is not my father."

"So, Dean must know. Is he coming back to school this year?"

"Yeah. We found out while we were on the windjammer cruise. Mure checked in with Mr. McKee when we 'called at a port'—that's what they say when you stop at towns in a ship. I was so excited and couldn't wait to see Dean and tell him."

"He must be so happy about it, too," I said.

"Oh, yeah, he is. And we're together and everything. It's great. But it's different too." Brandi paused, looking into space.

"Different? How?"

"I can't explain it. But it's different. I mean we still love each other and everything. I don't know. When I do, I'll let you know. Hey, I gotta go. I'm late. I promised Mure I'd have the car back so she can go to Portland."

"Don't speed. I'll call her and let her know you're on your way," I said. Brandi hugged me and was gone in a flash of tanned skin, white shorts, and pink top.

PART FIVE

1

School started, and, as usual, very soon it was almost as if there never had been a summer break. One of the essential areas of the school program called for a commitment to community service. Annually every student formulated a plan that included a service goal for the year. During October the school's partner company co-sponsored the state Race for Cancer, a nationwide event. Since October also was Cancer Awareness Month, the school administration tried to get as many students as possible involved in the race and in related projects.

The previous June a beloved softball coach had been diagnosed with breast cancer, underwent a mastectomy, and returned to school in September, openly and actively discussing the disease with the school community. Her forthrightness heightened people's awareness and instilled a spirit of action among students, teachers, and community members. The entire varsity softball team participated in the Race, raising a considerable amount of money for the cause.

Brandi decided to make cancer awareness her goal for the year. While she did not play softball, her involvement as wrestling manager put her in a position of familiarity with most of the coaches, and Mrs. Allenby was one of her favorites. She became active in some of the projects around school. As one of the editors of the school newspaper, she used her column to write a personal account of her experience with the intimate, insidious nature of the disease. I always made a point of reading the high school newspaper to keep up with former students, so I saw Brandi's article:

> "Together We Are Strong"
> I almost died because of cancer. No, I don't have cancer, nor am I recovering from it. So far, I'm healthy. Statistically, I don't need to begin worrying about getting it for at least ten years or so--actually, I may never get cancer, or I could anytime. My life was jeopardized because

my mother got cancer when she was only a teenager. That's not supposed to happen, but it did. One of the things I found out when I started learning more about cancer is that it doesn't happen in a way you can predict.

I was four years old when she died. I had no father and no other family. The social services placed me in a foster home when I was very small because my mother was too sick to take care of me. I was even adopted by one of the families. But it never worked out for me. I was not an easy kid to take care of, and stand-in parents lost patience with me.

I am a cancer survivor. Thanks to help from community agencies, money, and some caring people who worked very hard, even when I didn't think I wanted the help, I made it. These three ingredients are necessary for all cancer victims to become survivors.

I'll bet someone you love or know very well is battling cancer right now. You are the best person to help them and help conquer the dread and waste of this disease. We need your help right here in this school. There are many projects we are working on in the fight against cancer. We have things for everybody, no matter whether you have special talent or not. Some take only a little time. Please come to the guidance office and look at the different projects there are. Sign up for one or two, or even three or four.

You could save your own life and not even know it.

Brandi Buckman

Almost before I realized it, fall diminished into that period of cold, dark gray that encloses December. One Friday night my husband and I attended a wrestling meet at the high school. When we entered the gym, I saw Brandi at the scoring table.   Her chair was located toward the middle of the table, two other girls were sitting on one side of her, a man sat on the opposite side, and several members from both teams were standing around the table, talking animatedly. I decided to wait until after the meet to chat with her.

Dean had secured the varsity slot for his weight class that season.

When his turn came to wrestle, I was impressed with how much older--a man of nineteen now--he looked since I last had seen him in the winter. Over six feet tall, slender but muscular, with broad shoulders and rippling muscles visible in his upper back, arms, and legs--the parts of his body showing in the skimpy singlet wrestlers wear--he of the olive skin and black hair stood out attractively among the other, mostly pale-skinned and light-haired wrestlers. He appeared to be in excellent wrestling form, too, as I watched him pin his opponent in twenty seconds.

I knew through the grapevine that Dean was doing well in school and still living with Tom and Elizabeth Ryan.   As far as the gossip mill knew, he saw nothing of his father; nobody really knew whether he saw or spoke to his mother, A senior now, he would graduate in June and was applying to colleges that had wrestling programs.   With Coach Ryan's national reputation and his personal recommendation, there was a good chance that he might get a wrestling scholarship.

When the meet ended, I got an opportunity to say hello to Dean, who, after showering and changing, joined Brandi where she chatted with my husband and me in the hallway. "Congratulations," I greeted him. "I see you're doing great on the team."

"Thanks, Ms. M. Hello, Mr. M.   Yeah, I really like wrestling. It keeps me focused."

"Yeah, well, focus on this, Buddy. I'm starved," said Brandi. "Let's get a pizza. Hey, Ms. M., I forgot to tell you. I'm submitting this poem I did in writing class to Mr. Farrelli, and I was wonderin' if you'd take a look at it for me.   He said he wants to put together a booklet of the best ones. Tell me what you think--if I need to do anything or whatever. It's in my backpack."

While she was fumbling in her pack, Dean said, "She wants hers to be one of the best ones--it probably is the best. She's always scribbling away at something. She has more journals she's written than I have books of any kind."

Handing me the paper, she laughed. "Yeah, well, it's the only way I can keep my head straight. Com'on, let's go. See ya."

Over the weekend I read Brandi's poem, marveling at the development in her writing:

Faith: To Muriel

Out of the void
you found me
and rescued me from myself.

You saw, as I did not,
a heart beating, a desire that stirred,
beneath the hostility.

Black and gray mass, roiling,
in your patient tutelage
became silver form.

by Brandi Buckman

In our school system, wrestling traditionally has been one of the most successful varsity sports, in terms of championship victories. Under the coaching expertise of Tom Ryan, the team won the most state titles of any school during the years the activity existed at the school. To its credit, also because of Coach's dedication and charisma, the team was reputed to be a perfect place for troubled and at-risk teen-age boys to develop into upstanding student citizens.

The next time I made it to a wrestling meet was not until the finals, at the end of February. The varsity had wrestled an undefeated season, ranking first in its division. By virtue of having won the regional title, our high school hosted the state finals.

The state wrestling meet required most of a weekend to complete. Since it takes about eight hours to drive the length of Maine, bus loads of high school boys descended upon the community and, for the most part, were housed by parents and friends of the school. Some stayed in hotels, but usually the visiting parents, relatives, and supporters of the various teams filled these accommodations. Besides, there was a sense of camaraderie and festivity about the meet. Some of the players wrestled each other over the four year period of high school, developing friendships bridging the span of time between their meetings. For these boys, the weekend was a time of reunion.

The Booster Club, run by parents of present and past athletes, as well as other interested adults, worked for a couple of weeks before the scheduled date of the championships to set up adequate housing accommodations. After the announcement of teams qualifying and of the participating members, names of guests were matched to hosts. This year the number of participants was especially high because most slots for weight categories were filled. Often a school with a small team might not have enough members to fill all slots, so this year was unusual.

The gym was packed with myriad odors. There was the smell of sweat, of course, from the almost two hundred wrestlers, and from the several hundred supporters, some of whom expended as much energy as the boys. People generally were overdressed, having come into the overheated school from the frigid outdoors.

From the concession stands, run by the Boosters and various community organizations, emanated food smells: hot dogs, pop corn, meatballs in sauce, candy apples, cotton candy, even garlic, onions, and peppers. Some people brought coolers filled with things they prepared: Italian sandwiches, egg salad, cheese, fruit, whoopie pies, doughnuts, and gallons of soda, coffee, juice, and bottled water. Separately, the fragrances would be appetizing. Competing as they did with each other, they made the place smell more like a school cafeteria run amok. Despite the overall pungent odor that resulted, people consumed an amazing amount of food during the weekend. The spectators absorbed the smells and oozed them out into the gym.

Tension and excitement produced an odor, also. Most people had a son, a grandson, a nephew, or a friend competing. Those who didn't know any wrestler personally came because they enjoyed the scene, and they brought their own enthusiasm. To me, the place smelled something like overripe bananas or the compost pail I kept by the kitchen sink.

The season proved a particularly sweet one for Coach Ryan's team.

Besides hosting the State Championship, his boys won the meet with an impressive showing. Equally important to many people, the school team won the Good Sportsmanship Award, voted on by the coaches and awarded to the team displaying the overall best spirit of the games. Several team members won individual state titles, and Dean won this award for his weight class.

Because of Tom Ryan's national reputation as an Olympic wrestling assistant coach several years back, colleges paid attention to his teams and the boys he trained. Winning an individual state title as a member of Coach Ryan's team opened doors and could produce scholarships at several universities. Some of the seniors anticipated they would get into a school the following year with a wrestling scholarship. For Dean it was the only way he could hope to attend college.

3

The high school possessed strengths in some areas other than the wrestling program. One was the drama department. Before he started teaching high school, George Bouton had acted professionally, including a few times off-Broadway. After marriage and children, he moved to Maine to teach, although he often acted in community theater. Fans traveled around the area to watch George perform. The plays he directed at the high school always were first-rate; often the drama department competed at the annual state drama competition in the spring, and occasionally the plays won.

Brandi auditioned for, and won a part in, the spring production her junior year. "We're putting on "Hair." I'm so excited; I hope I can do a good job. Will you come to the play?"

"I won't miss it," I answered. "Sounds like fun."

The lead went to a junior who had acted in high school productions since his freshman year and in various community theater events for several years. Since "Hair" had a large cast, many students got the opportunity to test their thespian skills.

Excited to be acting, to be singing and dancing, as well, Brandi told me, "I don't know how good I'll be at singing, but Mrs.

Paulin says I can do it fine. She's going to help me after chorus so I can get my songs down. The dancing's gonna be unbelievable. There's this totally nude scene where nobody wears any clothes--I guess that's nude, duh. But we can't do it that way cuz of performing in school and stuff. So we're going to wear these body stockings, and the house will be real dark, and there'll be these strobe lights on us. It should be so totally amazing."

It was amazing. As usual Mr. Bouton produced a fine show, designing innovative staging, adding his own unique touches to scenes, and generating fine acting from his charges, some of whom had no idea of and little belief in their capacity to rise to the challenge. They put on a terrific performance, winning easily at the regional competition, and then going on to capture the state title.

Brandi shared in the thrill of a job well done. She had a fine singing voice, clear and true, and showed strong stage presence. I always knew she was something of a ham who enjoyed the limelight.

In April Dean received acceptance to college in Boston and was offered a generous wrestling scholarship. Remembering the punk I'd feared in middle school and the crazed, hateful teenager who'd terrorized an entire student body, I thought about how far he'd traveled since those years, as well as how, instead of planning to start college, he might be wasting his youth in prison, apprenticing to become a career criminal.

I sent Dean a card and a note expressing my delight over his good news.

A few days later, he appeared in my classroom at the end of the school day.

"Hi. Thanks for the nice card," he said.

"I'm so happy for you. It's nice of you to stop by."

"This is the first time I've been in the school in three years— since that day. It almost seems like that person was somebody else."

"It was you but not you, too. You've grown and changed."

"I'm so sorry I ever pulled such a stupid stunt."

"You should remember. It's an incentive to set goals. You've proved you're capable of achieving them." I paused and chuckled. "Now, listen to me--I sound like a teacher. You must be excited about college."

"Oh, I am--a little scared, though. I've never been out of Maine, except for the time Brandi and I went to Disneyland. The

Ryans and I are going up to Boston during spring vacation. I'm meeting the wrestling coach, and we're also gonna tour the city."

"Well, that should be fun. I have a feeling you'll do well."

"I think I'll do okay. Elizabeth said I should consider the alternative whenever I'm down."

"That was pretty direct."

"Yeah, well, she knows me inside out." He laughed. "We're going to go to Indiana for six weeks this summer to run a wrestling camp. I"ll be Coach's student assistant. There's a lot to learn that'll come in handy at college, and I'll earn some pretty good money, too. Everything's going to be great."

Dean's enthusiasm, like a dream that plays lightly on the fringes of reality, teased me that day.

4

Spring sometimes blessed Maine; mostly though, we experienced winter, mud season, and then summer slipped in, almost without our realizing it, while we were slopping through the mud. This particular year, however, we luxuriated in a glorious spring--sunny days, lovely evenings, mild temperatures, scant rainfall. First came all the flowers--crocus and trillium, then daffodils, azaleas, tulips, lilacs--and for once the blooms lasted long enough to die a natural death, rather than be knocked down or blown off by rain and wind or killed by a heavy blanket of slushy snow, in a last-ditch attempt by Mother Nature to show who was boss in Northern New England. As the evenings lengthened, we all spent more time outside in the warmer air, glad to put aside the heavy cloaks of winter.

That month the faculty named Brandi a representative to Girls' State from our high school. One of the biggest honors bestowed on a junior, Girls' State and Boys' State consisted of week-long conferences to teach young citizens about state government. Juniors from most schools in the state spent a week on a college campus, boys at one school and girls at another, learning how government runs by engaging in mock legislative activities.

I saw Brandi briefly before she left for Bangor and when she returned.

Prior to going, she was excited about experiencing a good time and a new situation. After her return, she was reflective. "It was amazing to be with so many girls for a whole week. I never dreamed there was so much to know about government and how laws are made. With all the reasons you can talk about why there should be a law or why there shouldn't and the amount of time it takes, it's a wonder a bill actually makes it into a law. But everybody takes the work so seriously--that's a good thing. Girls' State got me to thinking that maybe I'd like to be a lawyer."

"You'd make a good lawyer, I guess. But I thought you wanted to be a writer," I said.

"Well, yeah, I want to do that, too. But Mure said I could probably work in a law office this summer. She has connections with some lawyers, and she's going to get me lined up with one for a summer job. It probably will be doing stuff like filing and running around, sort of a handyman, law style. But at least I can see what they do and maybe go to court and stuff like that. "

"I'm sure it will keep you busy."

"Yeah, that's good, too. Dean's gonna be gone most of the summer, so I'm glad I'll be busy. Oh, speaking of writing, I want you to read something I wrote in my journal at Girls' State--thought you might be interested. I brought it with me."

Later I read the place Brandi had marked in her journal:

I met a girl from Frenchton. Melissa Dupree. Frenchton's a town way down on the Canada border, about eight hours from Portland. Melissa is an amazing person. I have so much respect for her. We told each other absolutely everything about our lives--we are so much alike, we could be sisters. We aren't sisters, of course, but some of the things we think, the way we feel about stuff, it's like we are soul sisters. It's also weird what's happened to both of us. We both had hard times—different reasons--but we both had a lot of help from someone who cared. And that's what saved us--her from being a welfare mother, me from being a druggie or in jail.

Melissa didn't have a father either, but she has her biological mother. When she was a kid her mother had a boyfriend they lived with. He was a creep who hit on her when her mother was at work and stuff. Donnie would hang around, but he would try to do things to her--she was about twelve then. I asked her why she didn't tell her mother and she said she started to but her mother didn't want to hear anything bad about Donnie. She said they were lucky to have a place to live because of him. Otherwise they would be in some room or something instead of a nice, warm house—actually it was a trailer, Melissa said, and not all that nice. But her mom didn't make much money, and Melissa knew she was right that they would have a much worse place to live. Although that would have been all right with her, but her mother also loved Donnie.

So finally one night her mother was at work and Donnie was drinking. Melissa was trying to study when he came in her room. He started smoothing her hair, kinda playing with it. Then he tried to touch her, and she said she couldn't stand it. She got away from him, ran out of the trailer, and left.

Melissa said she had a friend, a boy who was a little older, like 16, who always had been nice to her all her life. When she left her place she was scared and didn't know where to go. So she called Mickey and told him. He had been begging her to leave for a while--he had an aunt who said Melissa could stay with her. So they went to the aunt's house, and she stayed there.

When her mom found out, she tried to get Melissa to come home. But she still didn't believe that Donnie tried anything with her, so Melissa stayed at the aunt's. So anyway what happened was she and Mickey spent a lotta time together cuz he was always at his aunt's house--he slept there a lot too. Well, he was so nice to her and Melissa was so alone now--she didn't see her mother and she was sad and everything. Well, what happened was she got pregnant. She said that wasn't so bad--I would think it would be, but she didn't. That's one big difference between us, but she told me a lot of things about having a baby and all so now I am starting to see a different point of view. I still wouldn't want a baby now, but I can understand how somebody else might.

Anyway, Mickey was happy about it and said a baby would be nice—and they could get married if Melissa wanted to. Well, she was pretty mixed up, so they kinda just went along for a while. A couple months passed. Her mother found out and wanted Melissa to come back. She actually thought the baby was Donnie's--she finally believed Melissa about Donnie messing with her and she didn't believe that it wasn't his. In fact her mother moved out of his place and moved in with a girlfriend she'd met at work. They could afford a good enough place if they shared the rent.

Melissa was thinking about going back to her mother. She and Mickey argued about it a lot. One night they were driving in his truck and Mickey was yelling at her about staying with him. He wasn't paying attention to his driving and somehow they went off the road and down a steep bank, and the truck rolled over a couple times.

Melissa hardly got hurt, which was amazing. But Mickey was killed.

Melissa was so broken up about it cuz she blamed herself for the accident. She had made him so scared about her leaving. She also felt guilty because she was a little relieved that she didn't have to live with Mickey--and she said this part really made her feel horrible. How could she be glad someone who had been so good to her was dead--even if she hadn't loved him?

Well, her mom came and got her at the hospital. She had her baby—a little girl she called Michelle, named after Mickey. This part is so incredible. Michelle had a baby when she was 14 and now she's 17 like me, and she's finished her junior year and was picked to go to Girls' State. Everybody accepts what happened and doesn't judge her or anything. Her mom helps her take care of Michelle, who is almost 4 now. And Melissa says it's really a blessed life she has-- that's what she calls it--"a blessed life."

She showed me pictures of Michelle--she's so cute. She said her mom brings her to school sometimes, and everybody is so nice to her. They all love Michelle. And Melissa even has a boyfriend who doesn't care that she has a baby--a little kid now, actually.

I thought I had it hard. And I did. But Melissa showed me that lots of people have tough things happen to them, tougher than I did--though she thinks my story is tougher than hers. She calls the things that happened to us "our stories." We shouldn't wallow in misery and let things get us *down, she says. Everybody has a story but it shouldn't stop them from doing okay.*

I love Melissa.

5

June arrived, and with it, graduation. The student population at the high school had increased over the years so that the celebration no longer could be held indoors without limiting the number of guests. And every senior's grandmother wanted to watch her grandchild receive a diploma. The weather was too fickle to depend on an outdoor program, so graduation exercises were performed at the Community Center in Portland. The area was huge and impersonal, but students had no limit put on their guest list--brothers, sisters, friends, babies were all welcome.

After the ceremony, school buses pulled up outside the arena, and students boarded, to be transported to their previously chosen destination for an all-night chemical-free graduation party. Students weren't allowed to drive; they traveled together in the busses to one place to celebrate. Accidents, particularly those resulting from driving while drinking, declined to a fraction of what they had been in the past, before parents and friends instituted the idea of one big, chem-free blast. The Boosters Club raised money all year for the event and hired a disc jockey, served food, and ran casino games all night. They solicited donations and bought enough prizes so every senior got a few. The prizes included items like ipods, TVs, bikes, cameras, and sometimes a cell phone or even a car. Over the years the party had grown so popular that nearly all of the graduating seniors attended the event.

My husband and I sat with Muriel and the Ryans at this year's graduation. Brandi sat with her friends, mostly juniors who had brothers, sisters, girlfriends, or boyfriends graduating. Even in a place as devoid of atmosphere as a giant sports complex, the thrill of the moment took over. When some two hundred fifty, festive-looking seniors--boys dressed in green robes and girls in white robes--marched onto the floor, voices rose in cheers accompanied by clapping and the stamping of feet. I felt as excited as anyone, I think, happy for the completion of four years of high school for Dean and thrilled by the promise of a bright future for him.

At the end of the ceremony, spectators rushed out onto the floor to join the graduates in a massive wave. We moved from group to group congratulating my former students, shaking hands with their parents, and chatting with colleagues and friends. My husband and I saw Tom and Elizabeth Ryan with Dean and a few other students and headed in their direction. Before we reached them, we noticed an altercation nearby, at a door opening onto the street. Although we couldn't make out what was being said, we heard loud voices. Two security officers were speaking to a man; it looked as if they were trying to detain him.

Getting nearer, I realized the third man was Guy Muzzio. Dean saw him, too, because he left the group of well-wishers around him and strode toward the threesome, Coach Ryan close behind.

"You can't go in there, sir," the shorter security guard was saying, as my husband and I approached.

"Oh, yeah? My kid's in there. I have a right to be in there."

"No..." the bigger guard spoke, reaching out to grasp Guy's arm.

"It's okay," Dean said, coming up to the three men, with Coach right on his heels. "I'll talk to him."

"Well, well, the big star. This big star is my son," Guy said to no one in particular, maybe to the security guard who still held his arm in a firm grip.

"What are you doing here?" Dean asked. I could tell by the stiffness of his body and the flatness of his eyes that he was furious.

"Can't a father congratulate his own son on his graduation day? I came to congratulate you, boy," Guy slurred his words, and I realized he had been drinking. No surprise, I thought. He'd even try to wreck his son's celebration by barging uninvited.

"Well, you said it."

"You better go now," the shorter guard said to Guy.

"I have something to give my son."

"Sir, you can't stay here." I knew the guard was referring to Guy's condition. Alcohol, or any sign of it, was forbidden at the graduation site. Public drinking is illegal in Maine. And Guy reeked. If he wasn't drunk, he was well on his way.

"Come outside with me, boy. I want to give you something."

"Son, you go back to your friends. We can handle this," the shorter guard said.

"It's okay. I'll talk to him for a minute," Dean said. Because his jaw trembled slightly, I thought he must be pretty upset. I wondered if he also felt embarrassed that his father was causing a scene. I wanted to tell him he shouldn't think Guy Muzzio's bad behavior would be construed by anyone as a reflection on himself, but, dumbly, I didn't say anything.

"Are you sure? We can take care of this."

"No, it's okay."

"Com'on outside for a minute." Muzzio wheedled.

Tom Ryan stepped next to Dean. "I'll go with you," he said.

"No, it's okay, Coach. I can handle it. I'll be back in a minute."

Dean and Guy walked out the door onto Spuce Street. I silently cursed Guy Muzzio for interfering in Dean's special night.

The security guards moved off to deal with a couple of overexuberant graduates who were fooling around with some maintenance equipment, and the people who had been watching the interaction between Dean and his father talked to other graduates. The Ryans stood chatting with us until Muriel and Brandi appeared.

"Hi, everybody. Hey, where's Dean?" she asked.

"His father showed up, so he went outside to talk to him," I answered.

"He should be back any minute," said Elizabeth Ryan.

"Oh, shit." Brandi's grin turned into a scowl. Suddenly she grew agitated. "I need to get him. Guy's been like stalking him, showing up wherever he is ever since he found out Dean got the scholarship. He's such an ass--bugging Dean all the time. Where'd they go?"

"Just outside," Tom Ryan said. "Come on, we'll get him."

They went outside but returned a couple of minutes later. "They're not there. Get those two security guards. We need to find them." Tom looked worried.

Elizabeth, Muriel, my husband, and I stood on the sidewalk, looking up and down Spruce Street while Tom, the security officers, and Brandi spoke to two policemen who were standing by their patrol car, watching the school busses. While students boarded, parents, friends, and well-wishers milled around. The noise level disconcerted me: shouting, cheering, cat-calls, whistles, noisemakers; somebody even had some firecrackers. The police didn't look very happy about all the confusion. They reached one group of boys throwing water-filled balloons from a bus window at passing cars about the time I heard someone screaming, "Police. Someone. Help us. Call an ambulance."

I turned and saw Tom running from an alley behind the Community Center. Everything was a blur then. A lot more police must have been on duty around the civic center than I had noticed, as well as an ambulance on call for graduation. In no time, police mobbed the area. The ambulance, lights flashing, siren blaring, crawled through the mass of people.

I couldn't move; I couldn't extricate myself from the crowd.

Somebody yelled, "Back here. "

A policeman broke an opening for a couple of medics with a stretcher.

"Move out of the way, folks. Coming through." I fell into step behind a young, fair-skinned policeman. The alley turned a corner and dead-ended at a brick wall. A couple of blue dumpsters with "Fogg" stenciled in white, large cans, some broken metal staging, and lots of papers littered the vicinity. Near one of the dumpsters Brandi crouched over Dean, blood on his tee shirt and on the ground beside him. Tom Ryan took her shoulders and tried to pull her to her feet, but she was hanging on to Dean.

"Oh, my God," I whispered, reaching for my husband's hand.

"Help him, for crissake, somebody, please," Brandi appealed to the medic.

"Gunshot wound, "I heard the medic call out to his partner. Then they were moving around, quickly I guess, but to me it all happened in slow motion. Time hung suspended somewhere above the high brick walls, with the fragrances of the warm spring night conflicting with the stench of garbage.

"Clear a path. Get back, people. Stretcher coming through. Make way." More police arrived and pushed folks back and out of the way of the medics carrying Dean on the stretcher and moving rapidly toward the ambulance, partially backed into the alley now, lights flashing. Brandi was holding the side of the stretcher, half-running to keep up with the medics.

My husband and I were the last people to leave the alley, just ahead of two policemen. "There ain't no rush," I thought I heard one say to the other.

6

As things turned out, I had heard the medic correctly. There was no rush because Dean was dead.

His death changed a great many things--little things, like the cancellation of the all-night graduation party, an early closing of school for the undergraduates, and a complete sell-out of all available flowers at the two local florist shops. Big changes occurred, too: the school board voted to tighten security and limit the number of guests at all future functions, Tom and Elizabeth Ryan set up a memorial fund in Dean's name for local high school boys, and Brandi lost her abundant zest for life.

I saw her briefly before Muriel took her away for the summer. "This girl needs to heal," Muriel told me. "I just hope she can."

A couple of weeks after Dean's funeral, I stopped by Muriel's house to say goodbye to them. "Lord, Muriel," I said, out of Brandi's earshot, "she looks horrible. Do you think it's wise to take her on some trip now?"

"She's physically strong. It'll do her good, if anything can help. She's hardly stopped crying since that night. And she hasn't slept. I need to get her away from here. The phone doesn't stop ringing, people come by even when I tell them not to--oh, I don't mean you. She wants to see you--she asked me to have you come by."

"Hi, Brandi," I said. I stopped. I'd said all the sympathetic inanities I could think of at the services for Dean. We hugged each other for a long time, it seemed.

"Oh, Ms. M. It hurts so much."

We sat down with our arms around each other and didn't say anything for a while. Then she said, "I'm sorry. I can't talk. But I wanted you to take my journal and read it. I know you understand."

Excerpts from the journal revealed quite a tribute to Dean, as well as a compendium of Brandi's feelings. I reread portions:

> I don't know how I can go on. I don't know if I want to. How can there be a god who lets things like this happen? Oh Dean--oh it hurts so much. WHY? I told you to stay away from your father. You damn asshole--I hate you for letting him win. You know he wanted to hurt you--but I cant believe he really shot you.

I didn't believe him when he said he wouldn't let you turn your back on him. I cant believe we didn't take him seriously. Why didn't we? Oh, Dean Oh Dean You were worth a million of that horrible horrible excuse for a human being. I cant even write anymore right now

~~~~~~~

I will not let Guy Muzzio keep me from remembering you. I know if there is a heaven you are there now. And if there is a hell he will burn there. I hope hell is like that picture by that painter Bosch we saw. And Guy is suffering like he never did on earth. I know I'm supposed to be a Christian, but I am glad he's dead, and I hope he suffered a lot while he lay in that ditch bleeding from the bullets. I'm glad he pulled his gun on the cops when they tried to stop him, and I'm so glad they shot him. And I'm glad the ambulance didn't get there in time so he'll always have to limp around hell. And I don't care if God and the world think I'm not a Christian cuz I feel that way. I don't want to be a Christian in a world that lets something like that happen to you.

~~~~~~~

I can't seem to do anything besides cry. I'm so sick of crying--I'm so sick of myself. But everytime I try to think about anything, all I can think of is you   And it hurts so much then, that I dont want to think anymore and I just start crying again. Mure says I have to take control of myself. But I say why? What for? She says I will figure that out. She said I should have someone to talk to--a psychologist, someone who doesn't know me or Dean--somebody just to listen to me so I can get it all out of my system. She says I need to do this before I can start to heal. I said if it means I have to live in a world without you, I don't want to heal. I'd rather die. She says I'm not ready to take control of myself yet. I said I won't ever be ready. She says she can wait. I told her not to hold her breath. She says my snottiness is a good sign. Of what I said—my snottiness? And she said yeah. I think I might cry myself to death if it weren't for Mure.

~~~~~~~

I need to talk to you Dean. Are you listening? You better be. You had no right to leave me. I wasn't ready--Im not ready. I thought I had about 50 years at least. It's not fair. I hate the way things are. I've even thought about killing myself to be with you. I told Mure I want to die. She said it's probably natural but that Im being stupid. If I die too then Guy really wins. I told her I dont know what she means. She said she doesn't know exactly what she means either, but shes sure things happen for a purpose--that's how she lives her life. She got stuck with me at the Youth Center for a purpose and look at what happened. I told her don't try to be funny. It's not funny. And she said she's not being funny. She really believes she and I were destined to meet for a reason. Some of it was for her to raise me and some was for me to add meaning to her life. But she says there's more to it than that. And we have to play out our parts in the life we get. Well I know she maybe believes that, but I told her I don't really believe it. But I told her I won't kill myself without letting her know first. She said well that's a relief.

~~~~~~

Some geek from Mure's church came here and told me each day will get a little easier and I must trust in God's greater wisdom. I almost told the asshole to stick it up his ass, but Mure was staring at me and making this awful face so I didn't say anything. But after he left I told her if she lets any other yahoos like that try to give me any more bullshit I will tell them what I think whether she likes it or not. It's been weeks and it's not any easier---it's harder to get up every morning. I wake up with the sun shining in my bedroom window and think oh what a nice day and I feel good for a minute. Then I wake up all the way and I remember. And it's like I wish I could sink down to sleep again and never wake up.

~~~~~~

I wish I could turn things back to that last week before graduation. When we ran into Guy outside the video store, I knew he had been following Dean. And then Dean told me Guy'd stopped him before. I said he should tell Coach and have him call the police. Stupid, stupid. I never should have let Dean talk me out of telling about Guy. I was such a jerk. Dean was such a jerk. He thought he could take care of himself. And he could have too if that bastard hadn't got himself a gun. But we should have known he might do something like that. Guy knew he couldn't beat Dean in a fair fight so he would stoop to doing something dirty. It's so obvious now—how could we have been so dense? I think I knew something was wrong--why why why didn't I tell somebody. Stupid dumb jerk

~~~~~~

Mure says if I won't go to counseling then we are getting out of here for a while. First I said I wanted to stay here. I've been putting flowers on Dean's grave everyday. Mure said that's been okay but now I have to start to get on with my life. Dean would want me to. She says I can put a plant--actually she said I can plant a whole garden--on his grave if I want. But we are going away. I got mad at her and went to bed and wouldn't get up till the next day. But I couldn't sleep all that time and I thought. I thought about what Dean would want me to do. I asked him. I said well wise guy you left me here all alone. What in hell do you expect me to do? Silence. Shit, I said. You can't just leave me here like this. I tried to sleep but I kept seeing his face. It makes cry to know I can't ever touch that face again or kiss that silly grin or pull those beautiful curls. What in HELL am I supposed to do????? And I remembered that Dean said we should fill up our life with all the experiences we could. We had decided when he went to Boston and I was still in Maine that we wouldn't be like some of the couples who don't do anything cuz they are separated. We decided we would take advantage of all the opportunities that came along--friends, concerts, parties, whatever. It wouldn't mean we loved each other any less. It meant we wanted to be as interesting as we could be for each other. So I decided that meant I should have as many experiences as I can to make up for the fact that Dean can't contribute any more--I'm still mad about that, Buddy. But I'll go on that camping trip to Colorado and do Everything. And I will write about it all and tell you in minute detail, Dean-o. So minute that you go nuts cuz you have no choice but to listen to me since you got no place else to go.

Oh but will I ever be able to think about you without just bawling my eyes out? I miss you so much.

~~~~~~

When I knelt beside Dean in the alley he was still alive. He whispered what Guy said. Dean thought he was a big shot, but Guy was his father. He wouldn't let Dean forget he was Guy Muzzio's son and he wasn't leaving him. And then he shot him. I could tell Dean was hurt bad. He could barely talk. I told him to stop talking--an ambulance was coming and he'd be all right. I guess I thought he would even though I could see all the blood leaking from his chest. I told him to hold on. I told him I loved him. "Don't leave me Dean--I can't bear it if you do" I said. And he said, real soft, "I love you--I'll never stop loving you." And then he whispered something I'll never forget. "I have your heart--you have mine--always. Soulmates, Brandi."

I remember a poem we read in lit class, and it makes me think of us.

It's by John Keats.

"Fair youth, beneath the trees, thou canst not leave

Thy song, nor ever can those trees be bare;

Bold Lover, never, never canst thou kiss,

Though winning near the goal--yet, do not grieve;

> She cannot fade, though thou hast not thy
> bliss,
> For ever wilt thou love, and she be fair!"

I think Dean's like that lover in the poem. He can't ever kiss me or go to college or wrestle or marry me or grow old. He's forever 19. But he's forever happy cuz he's ready to do all those things. I'm like the girl too cuz always in my mind and my heart Dean is ready to kiss me. For ever wilt Dean love Brandi, and for ever she be his fair maiden. Like the people on the Grecian urn Dean and I forever are getting together--Guy couldn't take away our love.

This was what I loved about Brandi; she'd keep Dean alive by her strong memory. I wondered what else she might have to endure, though.

PART SIX

1

Five years before, I'd instinctively sensed a specialness about Brandi.

She stormed her way into my classroom, entering as an especially obnoxious pain in the neck and emerging as an individual. She possessed intelligence, wit, an engaging personality, and a keen sense for self-preservation. Countless obstacles might have thwarted her, yet she didn't allow herself the weakling's way out.

Brandi could have given up after Dean died. Nobody would have found fault if she quit her treadmill of activities, pronounced them extraneous to the fight for survival; after all, his death reflected a kind of futility in perseverance. He expended tremendous energy attempting to avoid that last confrontation with his father. Life comes with no guarantees, though; chance won't be accountable. Still, Brandi refused to quit and plunged directly into senior year, splashing herself around as if she had to make every drop count for both of them.

In her first election campaign, Brandi won the vice-presidency of the senior class. Her slogan, pitched on posters around school--"Squish the stuff of life between your fingers: Do Something"--grabbed student attention and peaked curiosity, just like an encounter with Brandi herself got people interested and then enticed them to come back for more of her engaging singularity. People became attracted to the aroma of her words, gathered to taste her personality, and remained because she offered them a feast of her vitality for life. I knew how it happened, because she'd done the same thing to me.

One day in late September I chatted with Brandi at a soccer game after school. "I've been to a couple of college visits. I have to get serious about this and write an essay. When I get it finished, will you look at it for me?"

"You know I will."

"Yeah, I know." She laughed. "Thanks, Ms. M. "

It was at least a month later that Brandi dropped by my classroom in her usual flurry. "Hey, Ms. M. What's up? Oh, guess what? I'm starting an internship with Mr. McKee--remember the lawyer who did my adoption? Well, it's part of the partnership in business thing the school does. I'm thinking about maybe going into law, so he's going to let me work with him. I'll even get paid a stipend--not much cuz we can't really be paid for internships, specially since we get to do them during school time."

"Sounds like it will be interesting. I'm amazed you have time for everything you're doing. I hear you even have a part in the fall play. Aren't you overextending yourself a little?

"The internship is only part of one day a week--not that much time."

Brandi eased herself into a chair off to the side of my desk. Sitting seemed to remove the starch that stiffened her body while erect. Now she slumped forward, elbows on the table, her face cupped in her hands. After a long pause where neither of us said anything, she spoke up. "You know, Ms. M., all this stuff--school work, the school paper, the play--that's the easy part. I'm doing great there. I'm even fifth in the class. It's really a relief to do homework when I get home at night. Studying keeps the demon in the shadows, ya know?"

"You mean thinking about Dean?"

"Yeah, I mean the ache never goes away. It's always in me--dull and soft, sort of, when I'm at school. And the busier I keep, the softer it is. Being around other kids, having people ask me to do things, that's good. But then when I have a minute by myself its like the pain demon is waiting, and that's when he pops me one in my gut or knifes me in the heart..."

She dropped her hands and lowered her head onto her arms. "Brandi," I said, closing the space between us. I eased into the seat next to her, attempting to encircle her with my arms. She turned, burrowing her head into my chest. I wrapped my arms around her upper body, caressing her back over the soft fuzziness of her sweater. We remained that way for several minutes, quiet except for her sobs. Eventually Brandi stopped crying and sat up; I reached for the box of tissues on my desk, took out a couple, and handed them to her.

"Oh," she sighed. "I guess I needed a little cry."

"You're very courageous."

"I don't feel courageous. Sometimes I think I'm occupying a space between the living and the dead, you know? I'm not really here or there. That demon haunts me."

"Do you mean you think about taking your life? I don't think..."

"Oh, no. I'd never kill myself. That would be an insult to Dean. Not to mention Mure--man, she'd kill me if I did that--except I'd already be dead--you know what I mean. But I don't mean I've never thought it would be easier just to give up, cuz I have. But I won't fall into that hell."

"That's good."

"I'm too much with me when I'm alone. I obsess about the memories. You know, I think the air might suffocate me. It's heavy and hot, like maple syrup; like I'm the pancake and the thick syrup slides slowly over me, seeping in and making my insides--my throat, my intestines, my stomach, my heart, especially my heart--limp, soggy, like I'll fall apart if anybody touches me. I have to fight the urge to give in and give up. Keeping busy is like a salve for my wounds. I slather all these things on me, and I push the demon away for a while."

"What about counseling?"

"I'm going now. Mure let me wait till I said I'd go--I couldn't talk about Dean to a stranger at first. If I even said his name it was like I had a little less of him left for me. I was afraid I'd pour out my heart and Dean would escape, and I'd be like an empty bottle. I'm not scared of that now. I know I'll never lose him--he's safe inside me forever."

"So the counseling helps?"

"Since it costs Mure fifty bucks a shot, I sure hope she's getting something for her money. Ha, ha. I'm making a joke. But, yeah, it helps. The psychologist sort of leads my mind certain ways, so I can understand myself better, I guess. But, you know, it's good to talk to you--to be able to just not think too carefully about what I'm saying. That's what I have to do--or I make myself do--when I'm with the counselor. It's never like just now, when I really lost it with you. I knew you'd understand, you know? You knew Dean. And that makes it, if not okay, at least easier."

"It's okay."

"I feel better now."

2

The next time I saw Brandi, she gave me the essay she had written for her college application:

College Essay

So what!   Another boring essay to plow through in the stack of applications by hopeful college wannabees. So, why is mine the one you should look at and exclaim, "Ah, yes, here it is-- the perfect essay by the perfect student?" Why should you care? What makes Brandi Buckman better than Joe or Carla or Bambi? I'm supposed to convince you.

Well, Brandi is not any better. Nope, I'm as good as the others, but I'm not any better. I don't always close the refrigerator door, frequently forget to feed the cat, occasionally drive too fast, and, worst of all, sometimes snap at my mom. That way I'm pretty average, I guess.

You have the list of my academic and extra-curricular achievements and the transcript of my courses, grades, and class rank. So I won't bore you further with that information. What don't those records tell you about me? Who am I and what do I think you should know about me so you invite me, instead of Bambi, to attend your college? Well, here goes:

It was a dark and stormy night, and I could have stopped a murder and I didn't. But I did save a baby from the dumpster behind Dunkin' Donuts, and I couldn't have done both. It was one or the other. Besides, saving the baby wasn't much of a risk--saving the chick being knifed would have been tricky. If I'd done that, you might not be reading this essay. Good for you, you may be saying, maybe, but not so good for me.

So, I hung out a lot around Dunkin' Donuts the winter I was twelve-going-on-thirteen. I'd run away from still another set of surrogate parents; I was glad to get away for a while, and they were glad to have the respite--I wasn't a very nice kid in those days. I'm not sure I'm that great now, either, but people seem to like my company better these days.

Anyway, on this dark--no moon--and stormy--snow and sleet--night—about 11:30 p.m.--I happened to be scooched down behind the D.D. dumpster, kinda wedged in a corner between some cardboard packing boxes and the brick wall of an apartment building. What was I doing there, you might ask--even if you don't, I'll tell you. Actually, there were three reasons:

1. I wanted a smoke real bad, and they don't let street kids smoke in D.D.--actually they don't let any kids, any adults, either, these days. There's a no smoking law in my state now, and, in fact, D.D. isn't there anymore, either. But I digress...I went to this spot to smoke a cigarette where nobody would see me and nobody would try to bum a drag.

2. I was out past curfew. Okay, now this is kind of involved, but I'll make it the short version. The cops leave runaways alone during the day, but we're supposed to be in the shelter by 10 p.m.--unwritten law the cops made up. If they catch you on the street after the witching time, they throw you in the holding cell at the jail--it is a warm spot, granted, but all the winos really smell and some get sick, and all in all it's not a nice place to spend the night. So I was avoiding the cops.

3. I also was hiding out from a mean dude intent on exacting revenge on me for... Well, this

gets very personal and would take too long to tell and I'd never get to finish about the murder and the baby. I hid behind the dumpster, hoping the dude wouldn't look for me there.

I had just taken a drag and was enjoying the sensation when I heard somebody approaching the dumpster. I snubbed out the cigarette and hunkered down. I heard a guy's voice and someone, female I thought, sort of sniffling. They stopped right on the other side of the dumpster, so I could hear them really well now. The guy sounded mad. He said something, and she started to cry. Then he hit her--I heard the unmistakable sound of a hand hitting flesh-- believe me, I know from experience what that sound is. It used to be in my dreams, nightmares, actually, but again I am digressing...

Then I heard a baby cry. She must have been holding it, and the slap and her crying woke it up or something. Well, he got madder--sort of yelling but in a kind of loud whisper like when you don't want anybody to hear you. He told her to shut the baby up. He must have been drinking. I heard noises--gurgling like when you tip a bottle to your mouth, smacking of lips, her say no, more gurgling. Then he asked did she have the bag. She answered yeah, but did they have to do it. And he hit her again and said something about how they'd been through it all and yeah they did have to do it. "Put it in the bag and let's get the hell out of here." I remember those were his exact words.

Well, apparently she changed her mind because she was crying more and saying she couldn't do it. So he said he would. And then things got crazy. He was slamming her against the dumpster, the baby was yelling--it must have been a really young baby, I thought, because, even yelling, its noise wasn't all that loud. The racket the guy and the woman were making was a lot louder.

I thought about jumping out from my hiding place and helping the woman. But I'd been on the street long enough by then to know that I would be no match for a drunk street guy who's angry. And just by the way she was acting--crying and begging and not fighting back--I knew she'd be no help to either of us. So I stayed put and waited.

He must have put the baby in the bag because its crying sounded more distant than before. Then I heard the sound of something being tossed into the dumpster--a kind of thump. And she started to scream, "No, no."

Well, what happened next I figured out after he left and I came out and looked at her. He must have had a knife on him. Either she didn't know or she knew and didn't think he'd use it on her. But he did. He cut her throat. I almost freaked when I saw her. I couldn't get out of there fast enough.

But first I did have the presence of mind to hoist myself up, reach into the dumpster, and feel around for the bag. Finally--it seemed to take me a long time, I was so scared the guy would come back or somebody else, a cop maybe, would appear and think I knifed the woman--I felt the bag and pulled it out of the dumpster. I opened it and reached for the baby. It didn't even have any clothes on--I didn't know right then, but I found out after that it was a newborn.

Anyway, I thought, forget the curfew, this is a matter of living and dying, and I ran out to Center Street and started yelling for a cop. Usually they're all over you when you don't want them. This time I couldn't find one. I had tucked the baby down inside my jacket, underneath my shirt and stuff--right against my skin, hoping it would stay warm enough.

Finally, a patrol car came along and I ran right out into the street to stop it. For once that night, something went right. Mike, my buddy, the best cop in Portland, was driving the police car, so I didn't have to explain myself. He knows me really well and knew I wouldn't have a baby or cut somebody or anything. I just pulled the baby out of my jacket and told him there was a woman, hurt bad, maybe even dead, by the dumpster. They took care of the rest.

So, on that dark and stormy night, I let a woman get murdered, but I saved a baby's life. You won't find this information in my school records, and I thought you might find it more interesting reading than the usual college application essay they tell you to write in the guidebooks for getting into colleges.

If you hung on this long, thank you for reading my essay, and I hope you'll let me into your fine college.

Yours sincerely,
Brandi Buckman

3

During the winter of her senior year, Brandi kept so busy that I rarely ran into her. She had given up the job of varsity wrestling manager. She felt sorry that she did not follow through in the activity, but she told Coach Ryan, "I can't walk into that gym without seeing Dean. Wrestling is Dean to me. It cuts me to my bones to be anywhere around wrestling. Maybe that will change. I hope so. But for now I have to stay far away."

One day a week she drove into Portland to work as an intern in the law offices of Brian McKee. She earned academic credit and a small stipend and an introduction to the business of lawyering: attorneys, briefs, courtrooms, and clients.

When I talked to her about it after she'd been there a month or so, Brandi waxed eloquent on the subject. "It's so cool, Ms. M., really. What a neat place to work. I feel like an adult. Some of the clients think I'm an assistant. One--I admit he's pretty vacant, but still, it was nice—even thought I was a paralegal. I've been to court with Mr. McKee once--I'm supposed to call him Brian, but I feel funny. He's old enough to be my grandfather, practically."

Brian McKee probably was fifty, not all that old to some people. "Anyway, I love the courtroom. It's so la-de-da. You have to be quiet and act just so. I get to carry papers and look important. I love it."

"That's terrific. Do you think the profession interests you, then, as a career for yourself?"

"Well, yeah, I think so. I mean I know it's a long way in the future, four years of college and then law school. Wow! But Mure says, 'Take it one step at a time. Get into college first, then see what happens.' She's right. Four years is a long time, and I might decide on something else."

"You're interested in writing too, aren't you?"

"Yeah, I want to be a writer, too. I don't know if I want to do that all the time, though. But I definitely want to take creative writing courses in college."

The next time I remember talking to Brandi she called me on the phone one evening in April. "I just got home, and I had to tell you first. I mean Mure knows--she sorta knew before I did cuz she was home and saw the big envelopes--but you're the first person I've called. I got into all three schools I applied to. Holy cow. I'm going to college. I'm so totally blown away."

"Well, congratulations. I'm not as surprised as you are though. I think they know a good thing when they see it—her I mean," I said and laughed.

"Yeah, well, thanks. I'm going up to Boston in a week to visit. There'll be other girls who've been accepted going, too; so I'll get to meet some of them."

"So you picked the all girls' school?" I asked, knowing it was the only one she had applied to that was located in the Boston area.

"Oh, yeah, totally. I don't need a bunch of guys around to prove anything. Anyway, the city is there if I want some social action. Oh, I almost forgot. It's a really big deal, too. I got a huge scholarship. Isn't that great? Now Mure won't have to go to the poorhouse, and I won't have to take out any loans if I get a small job for spending money. Hey, I gotta go. Another call's coming in. But I wanted you to know. And thanks, Ms. M."

"For what? You did it yourself."

"Yeah, well, for lookin' at my essay and stuff. And telling me I should apply to colleges and everything. Just thanks."

"You're welcome."

As I set the phone receiver in its cradle, my mouth slid into a Cheshire cat grin. She'd really succeeded in turning her life around, and she deserved the rewards.

4

As graduation approached, I heard about the plans through the school gossip line. The changes the administration instituted resulted directly from Dean's death the year before, and I wondered how the reminder affected Brandi. Instead of a wide-open, everybody's welcome ceremony at the Community Center, graduation exercises were going to be tightly controlled in the school auditorium. Each senior had three tickets for guests. Then students could sign up for additional seating, if it became available. Teachers could bypass the formal invitation rule by volunteering to chaperone, so I added my husband's and my names to the list early, knowing I definitely didn't want to miss Brandi's graduation.

All administrators intended to be present, along with many faculty chaperones, the school police, security forces hired by the school board, and school board members. The strict control surely would stifle some of the gaiety of the event; it was a tough decision, and the school board chose safety first.

As a consolation to students who wouldn't be able to have all family members attend the ceremony, the school board voted to reinstate a modification of the old Baccalaureate ceremony. They had abandoned the Sunday service several years before.

Memory Day, the new program, would consist of a secular ceremony, including reminiscences by students and a video produced from slides and photos of the seniors, supplied by parents, friends, and school files. The administration thought that relatives and friends living in the community might attend Memory Day and feel less frustrated if they couldn't get a ticket for graduation itself. They planned to hold the function outdoors on the school grounds, with refreshments served by roving underclass students. In the event of inclement weather, the program would go on in the auditorium. In either case, the media department would run the video show in the gym.

The class officers voted to have Brandi represent them as a speaker. As it turned out, the sun shone over a lovely Maine day, "the finest kind," as old-timers called it--brilliant sun, low humidity, gentle breeze, comfortable temperature. Chatting among the audience ceased when Brandi rose from her seat and walked to the improvised stage set up on the fenced-in soccer field.

Standing at the podium, she looked beautiful. The blue of her dress enhanced her eyes, which seemed brighter today. The dress itself was an understatement of teenage sophistication, high school graduation style. Of a slick, thin material, the long skirt floated below a high bodice, with a slightly scooped neck, puffed sleeves cut cross-wise by thin satin ribbon to make double pouffes, and the same blue ribbon crossed over the front of the bodice. Her hair fell below her shoulders in loose waves; she had tied more of the satin ribbon around her head, Pocohantas fashion, ending in a bow with long streamers down the back. She'd completed the effect of some storybook-type character with a pair of ballerina slippers, pink nail polish, and slick lip gloss. The image defied me to call up that distant memory of Brandi the bitch girl beating up another punk in the middle of the school. She was still a strong, feisty, independent young woman, but this vision bespoke femininity, gentleness, and fragility, as well.

Brandi's speech fell somewhere between the two extremes. Her voice was strong and clear:

Hi, Everyone. For those guests who don't know me, my name is Brandi Buckman. I hoped to be speaking here today, Memory Day, because this school is the place that holds so many treasured memories for me. I'm sure it is the same for most of the seniors. So many events of our teenage years happened at school. We came here for four years not only to attend classes. We came to meet people, to socialize, to work on community projects, to participate in sports, and to share ourselves.

Now this is goodbye and hello.

Today ends our high school experience. We leave teachers, friends, activities, the building itself.   Some of us also are leaving our family, our home, and our community. So goodbye to yesterday. We are sad and contemplative. We are leaving the security of the known world for the insecurity of the unknown. We do so with courage and dignity. We are eager.

We also are preparing today to greet our future. Some of us are going to school, others are taking a job, some are going into the services, and others are getting married.   So hello to tomorrow. We are excited and scared, but we are ready to meet our new challenges.

I think people anticipated that Brandi would talk about Dean in her speech. That she chose not to told me she now kept him close to her, in her heart.

5

After completing her internship with Brian McKee and his partners, Brandi was hired to work a few hours a week in their offices.   During the summer she worked nearly full time. I knew she was trying to earn as much money as possible, so she would not have to work too many hours her first semester at college.

I was in town one day in July and dropped by the offices to say hello to her. The receptionist led me down a carpeted hallway to a small room with a window overlooking City Park. Brandi was flipping through papers on the desk and jumped up when she saw me. "Oh, hi, Ms. M. It's nice to see you. What're you doing here?"

"Hi, yourself," I said. "I'm in town to do some errands, and I thought I'd see if by any chance you might be free for lunch. I can adjust my schedule around yours."

"Oh, that sounds great. Actually, I can leave right now, if you're ready, that is."

"Sounds good."

She reached under her desk, hauled out a large shoulder pack, stuffed some papers and a notebook into it, slung it over her shoulder, and stood up. "Okay, let's go," she said.

Over lunch at a little restaurant on Bank Street, we chatted about things we were doing that summer and Brandi's anticipated departure for school at the beginning of September. We rushed through the meal because the restaurant was packed, service consequently was slow, and Brandi had to get back to the office since she was accompanying one of the lawyers to court that afternoon.

Walking back toward the law office, Brandi spoke. "I have something really, really important--momentous, actually--to share with you. But I didn't say anything at lunch cuz there wasn't gonna be enough time to tell it all to you. So. I brought my trusty journal with me--thought you could take it home and read it. Then we can talk about it, okay?"

"Okay, Brandi," I said. "That sounds fine."

After I arrived home, I settled into a chair and read Brandi's journal where she had marked it:

> Working in a law office has its advantages--especially if the office handles adoptions--and especially if the office handled your own adoption. Wow! Did I find out some incredible news.
>
> I was working on some files for Mr. McKee--Brian--in his office. He had a lot of stuff

that needed to be organized and put into the correct places in the file. Some of the papers were from recent cases, but a few were from old ones. Most of his records are organized by year and then alphabetized.

Well, I was just going along--it gets pretty boring after a while cuz it's not anything that challenges the old noggin. But I look at the names and make up stuff about the people or sometimes read some of the file if I'm really bored. I don't know if I should be doing that, but Brian never said I couldn't so I figure just a little peek now and then won't hurt. I'm not going to do anything with the information--tell anybody or anything.

Anyway, I had a file that went back a couple of years or so. So I got the right file cabinet, then I looked at the name--Duplessis. I found Duplessis in the file folders, stuck the papers in the case folder, and noticed the name Dupree right after Duplessis.

Huh, I thought to myself. That's Melissa's name, from Frenchton. I wonder if this case has anything to do with Melissa or her baby. I admit, I was being nosy. So, I opened the file and--knock me over with a feather--I see Muriel's name on a page. I flip some more, and I see MY name. Then I realize that this file is MY case file--I can't believe it. I pull it out of the file cabinet, sit down on the floor, and start reading.

I didn't stop until I'd read the whole file. I guess I was pretty absorbed in it and kinda crying too. Next thing I know Brian is kneeling on the floor beside me holding a Kleenex box. I didn't even think about being embarrassed or anything about snooping through his files--I just took a Kleenex out of the box, wiped my face, blew my nose, and sniffed. Then I looked at him, and I was going to say sorry or something, but he spoke first.

"Well, I'm glad you read that, Brandi. Muriel and I weren't sure when was the best time for you to be given all this information. So you made the job easier for us," All I could think to say was Oh. Then he said you may want to digest it all first, but if you want to talk about any of it, fire away.

So, I said first, my father's name was Pete Dupree. Like, duh. Really brilliant, Brandi. You already know that from reading, dummy. And he just said yes, that's right. He died in an accident before you were born. Where was he from, I asked. I already knew that answer too from reading the file, but I wanted him to say it. He was from Frenchton, Brandi. That's....

I know where Frenchton is. I know someone from there.

Oh, he said, you do?

Yes, I said, I met a girl at Girls' State from Frenchton, and we're friends. Her name is Melissa Dupree. After I said her name I looked at Brian.

He looked back at me funny-like. I didn't know that. Never thought about the last name much. I don't know why we didn't tell you before—just didn't seem important at the time. You'd had so many names that one more would have just been confusing.

Well it's not really my name, I said. They weren't married. No that's not true Brandi, he said. They were married. I found documentation of their marriage taking place in New Hampshire.

But nobody ever told me.

Well, maybe nobody besides your mother knew. They were married only a couple of days before his accident. After he died, perhaps your mother thought it better not to say anything. Maybe she was afraid. Maybe it was connected with the fact he was Down East when the accident occurred. I don't know why. We'll probably never know that part.

Then he was quiet for a minute. Hmm, he said next. This could be just a coincidence. Dupree is a pretty common name, especially down that way. But I wonder...

Yeah, I said. I wonder too, if you're wondering the same thing I am, that is.

Well I think there might be enough information in the file to find out if your father was any relation to the Dupree family this friend of yours in Frenchton belongs to.

That's just what I was wondering. Do you think we can find out? I asked.

Of course we can try, Brandi, he said. In fact, I can start making some phone calls right now. Do you have Melissa's address and phone, her father's name and address?

She doesn't have a father. Her mother never got married. Dupree is her mother's name. And Melissa lives with her mother.

Well, that may make it easier. Let's see what we can find out about this.

So, Brian made some phone calls to some officials in Frenchton. Then he called Melissa's mother and talked a long time to her. Well, the amazing thing is that Melissa's mother, Paula Dupree, and my father, Peter Dupree, were Sister and Brother!! And that makes Melissa and me COUSINS!!! All I could say to Brian when he figured it all out was no wonder we're soul sisters. It all makes sense to me now how we could feel so close right after meeting each other.

Well, the best part is I'm going to get to see Melissa. Brian is so unbelievably awesome. It was his idea totally. He asked Ms. Dupree, Aunt Paula (it sounds so weird, but it sounds neat too) if it would be possible to set up a visit with her and Melissa and him, and my mother and me. She said yes and he said he'd get back to her.

So I asked Mure. Brian said she might not like the idea so he wanted her to know everything before he actually set up a visit. But I told him I knew Mure would be glad. And she was. She knows I love her better than anybody in the world--I could say that even when Dean was alive because it's a different kind of love. She's as excited as I am to meet Paula Dupree and see Melissa--well, probably not as much as me, but she really wants to.

We're going down to Frenchton next week. I can't wait.

As soon as I finished reading, I called Brandi. She answered the phone and said, "God, Ms. M. What took you so long? I've been sitting here waiting for you to call. What do you think--isn't this the most incredible thing?"

"I think it's wonderful. Now you know who your father was, and you even have two relatives."

"Three. Don't forget Michelle, Melissa's daughter. Yeah, an aunt, a cousin, and a niece--I already know my cousin, and I love her. I really wondered for a long time what kind of father I had. You know, not so much that he was alive or anything, but just mostly if he was a nice person. Like when I thought maybe Guy Muzzio was my father, I almost got sick just thinking about that possibility. Now I can find out about him--maybe see a picture of him or something."

"It sounds great," I said. "Will you stay in Frenchton very long?"

"We don't have all the details worked out yet. Mure has time, and I can take as long as I want, Brian said. He has a few days, and he has some stuff to do down there anyway--I don't know if he really does or he just doesn't want us to think we have to go there and leave in one day."

"Well, I'm thrilled for you. Keep me posted, okay?"

"Yup, I will. I'm bringing my camera to take pictures, so I'll show you what Melissa looks like when I get back."

So, I thought, another fragment fits into place. Over a period of several years, Brandi had grown from a line of graffiti I found scribbled on a bathroom wall to a special young friend owning a piece of my heart.

6

I said farewell to Brandi at the end of the summer. Of course, I heard from her after she started college; periodically either Muriel or she would contact me to provide an update on her activities. Toward the Christmas holidays, I received a package in the mail. Inside was a loose-leaf notebook of brown leather with my name embossed in gold on the front. Brandi had scotch-taped an envelope on the cover. I opened it and read the letter inside:

> Hi, Ms. M.,
>
> You always told me how important it is to keep a personal journal. I used to think it was a waste of time, stupid even, when I first tried. But it's become a great friend, especially in times of need. I don't know how I would have endured the misery when I thought Dean's father was mine too, or when Dean died. I poured my heart out to my journal and it kept me sane--well, as sane as I can

be. I look at it every so often, and it keeps the memories alive for me. Not that I'd ever forget Dean--or a lot of other things, too--but all the details are in the journal, and I can see the whole picture when I read. It's hard to believe I was that crazy kid in middle school. Sometimes I forget how bad I was then--how bad things were for me too. I'm pretty lucky I didn't end up in the Youth Center again or jail--it's amazing I ever thought Mure wasn't the greatest person. Anytime I want to see where I'm going I just have to look back at where I came from.

So I wanted to send you a special present-- I'm a college woman now, and I want to remember this year always. You are one of the people who made it possible for me to get here. I decided when I started college I'd keep a journal. I don't write everyday and I don't put down everything. But enough. This notebook contains a copy of what's in my own journal so far. It's loose-leaf so when I send you another installment you can add it to the notebook.

I hope you like the idea--you may get pretty sick of this after a while and regret ever encouraging me to keep a journal! That would be pretty funny. See, I also thought that this way, I'm always there--you can't get rid of me. You can open the notebook anytime and like--Here I am!